Frozen

Rage

ALSO BY STEVE MCHUGH

The Hellequin Chronicles

Crimes Against Magic
Born of Hatred
With Silent Screams
Prison of Hope
Lies Ripped Open
Promise of Wrath
Scorched Shadows
Infamous Reign

The Avalon Chronicles

A Glimmer of Hope
A Flicker of Steel
A Thunder of War
Hunted

The Rebellion Chronicles

Sorcery Reborn
Death Unleashed
Horsemen's War

CONTENTS

Cover illustration by Shawn T. King

FROZEN RAGE

A Hellequin Chronicles Novella

By Steve McHugh

Frozen Rage takes place between the following two Hellequin Chronicles books: Promise of Wrath and Scorched Shadows.

For everyone who just needs to escape from reality
for a few hours.

CHAPTER ONE

THE REALM OF DREICH.

I was pretty sure I'd made a terrible decision to come here.

"No, fuck you," the large man bellowed, getting to his feet at one end of the table laden with food and drink. He pointed a long finger at the man sat at the opposite end, thirty feet away. If I was honest, it could have been three times that, and it still wouldn't have been long enough.

Tommy Carpenter, my best friend, stood beside me and sighed as he stroked his long, dark beard. A sure sign he was beginning to lose his patience. "I really wish I'd stayed at home," he muttered under his breath.

Thirty people sat around a table designed for twice that number, although the shouting match between the two men at the opposing ends had everyone else move back from where they'd been seated.

The hall we were in was designed to look like something from a European palace, with high ceilings where murals of various gods—some of whom I couldn't have named if I'd tried—looked like they'd stepped off the pages of a fashion magazine. The walls were adorned with paintings, several of which I was almost sure were from masters of the craft back on the Earth Realm. At least one was an original Michelangelo, and I wondered from where they'd been stolen. The stained-glass windows that ran along one wall let in rainbows of color that bounced off the highly polished wooden floor.

"It's fucking Shakespearean," Remy said from the other side of me. "Maybe they'll murder one another, and we could all stop pretending we care."

As far as ideas went, it wasn't the worst I'd heard recently.

"Well, it is a wedding," Diana said from the other side of Remy. "It's probably not a proper wedding until at least one person has been bludgeoned with something."

"You go to some weird ass weddings," Remy said, looking up at her.

Remy was a three-and-a-half-foot tall fox-man. He'd pissed off the wrong witch coven, and they'd tried to kill him by turning him into a fox. Clearly, it hadn't worked but the witches had all died, and their lives had been poured into a newly fox-man shaped Remy. He dealt with it by swearing and threatening to stab people. To be honest, as far as coping mechanisms went, I'd heard worse.

The two men were now face to face, spewing insults about each other's mothers, fathers, and at one point a particularly inventive curse about a goat and a block of cheese.

"When do we step in?" Diana asked.

Tommy sighed. Like half the people sat at the table, he was a werewolf, although he was probably stronger than any of them, and certainly less likely to pick a fight at a wedding brunch with the father of the bride.

Werelions made up the other half of the guests. There was a long and unpleasant history between the two species, mostly involving vast numbers of murders. Peace had been brokered for a few centuries but that hadn't stopped either side trying to tear the other in half whenever the chance arose. Some don't forgive or forget, and some are just arseholes. The father of the bride and uncle of the groom most certainly fell into those categories.

An apple was thrown, and it smashed against the wall beside Diana's head. Diana hadn't even flinched, she just slowly turned to look at the remains of the destroyed fruit, and then back at the no longer arguing families. All eyes rested on her.

Diana was half werebear, and not someone you wanted to anger unless you liked the idea of having your arms ripped off so she could beat you to death with them.

My mind cycled through options of what was going to happen next when I spotted the expression of glee on Remy's face.

The doors to the dining hall were thrown open. "Enough," a large man bellowed as he stormed inside. He had a dark bushy beard, was broad shouldered with bulging muscles on his arms, and a barrel chest. Long, dark hair flowed over his shoulders. He couldn't have looked less like the romanticized version of a Viking if he'd been pulled into the room while standing on a long boat.

"I'm going outside," I said. "Come get me if they start to throw anything more dangerous than fruit."

Tommy clapped me on the shoulder, and I left through a side exit usually reserved for the staff. The castle was on theme with the dining hall, designed to resemble something from the Middle Ages, if not earlier, but it was a much more modern piece of architecture. Even so, there were several secret passages for staff to use, and on more than one occasion as I walked the long hallway—adorned with old water color paintings of wars, and a carpet that I was pretty sure was thick enough to lose yourself in if you stood still for too long—one of the larger paintings was pushed open and several members of staff emerged. Most wore an expression of *oh crap* on their face as they presumably tried to remember if I was one of the arseholes fighting in the dining hall.

As I exited the castle, nodding to the two guards directly outside the main entrance, I walked through the large courtyard to the sound of horses neighing in the distance. It had been snowing on and off for the twelve hours since I'd arrived in the realm, and while there were runes inscribed in the stone exterior of the castle to ensure the snow never built too high, there was still a satisfying crunch where my thick boots punched through the soft layer.

A large granite water feature sat in the center of the courtyard, depicting a sword in the stone. Water bubbled from the sword hilt, streaming down into bowl beneath the statue. I smiled as I walked past. I'd seen Excalibur many centuries earlier, before it was lost, and I don't remember its hilt being quite so bejeweled.

After the courtyard, where there were more guards, I headed through part of small village that encircled the castle and separated the makeshift from the real. The village, like the castle, had been purposefully-built, although the people who lived here were the workers and caretakers, so in that respect it was a real working village. But it was still designed to look hundreds of years older than it actually was. The village was surrounded by a forty-foot high, grey stone wall. The only way out was through the portcullis and across the drawbridge. As I strolled beneath the portcullis and across the dark wooden bridge, I noticed the crystal-clear water that made up the moat wasn't particularly deep, yet it was all part of the facade of the place.

At the end of the drawbridge, was a huge stone archway, and I found one of the guests from the little soiree. He was sat on a stone bench, looking out into the thick forest. Mountains, forests, and lakes made up about eighty percent of the entire realm, which was probably one of the reasons why it had never boasted a large population.

A light wooden walking stick leaned against the man's leg, and he looked up at me and smiled.

"Gordon," I said.

He got to his feet and hugged me. "Nate, I didn't know you were here," he said before re-taking his seat.

"Tommy roped a few of us in to help with security," I said, settling beside him. "Nice beard," I said. "Distinguished."

"You've grown one too," Gordon said with a smile, stroking his own bushy yet greying beard—being a werewolf certainly had its advantages in the beard-growing department.

I rubbed my short growth. "Laziness," I said with a smile. "How's things?"

"Not too bad," he said. "Hera took London, and I hear you and Mordred fought a dragon, destroying part of the city in the process."

"A small part," I said with a smile. It had been just over a year since Hera had claimed London as her own, and, if I was honest, it had been a year of peace. I, like many of my friends and allies, was forbidden from returning to London on pain of death, but Hera had needed to spend time getting her stuff sorted, and with Arthur waking from his centuries long coma, it appeared she'd been forced to take a pause and behave. At least for now. It was unlikely to last, but I'd long since learned that you took your good times where you could.

"So, how did Tommy rope you into this?" Gordon asked.

"Ah, he said I needed something to do," I told him. "Apparently, taking some time away from destruction and mayhem is being lazy."

"Considering how much of your life has been destruction and mayhem, maybe he had a point," Gordon said with a smile.

"Well, this is anything but boring." I motioned to the castle. "This whole realm is batshit crazy."

"A hundred years ago, this whole realm was uninhabitable," he said. "I don't know who came up with the idea to turn it into a rich person's getaway, but I'm pretty sure they were rich."

"It must be nice for the people who live here all year around through," I said. "An entire realm for a thousand people for nine months of the year, and only having to put up with people like the wedding party for three months."

"It would be nice if it didn't rain for seven months of the year, and then snow for the rest of it. I think warm days here make up about a week in the year."

"Sounds like Yorkshire," I said, and we both laughed.

"I'm going to tell Matthew you said that," Gordon told me, his smile at the mention of his pack alpha husband, growing wider. "He grew up there."

"Where is Matthew?"

"He likes to go for an evening run before the sun goes down," Gordon said. "The snow gets heavier at night. The runes all around the village and castle make sure we don't wake up with six feet of snow, but out there it'll be different. Matthew didn't know when he'd get the chance for another run."

"You not joining him?" I asked.

"I don't need the run as badly as he does," Gordon said. "Never have. I'm more content to curl up in front of a fire with a good book. Matthew prefers to run until his heart feels like it's going to burst."

We sat in silence for a moment, enjoying the peace. "How long have you known the bride, or groom, or whichever one it is you know?" I asked, somewhat regretting that I had to break the tranquility.

"Bride," he said. "She's a descendent from the werewolf royalty who signed the pact stopping hostilities with the werelions. The royal family doesn't exist anymore, primarily because everyone just decided to ignore them and go about their business, but it's still a formality that they invite several alphas to their weddings, or funerals, or brunch. Matthew is one of the most powerful alphas in Western Europe, so we get the invite. There are about a dozen of them. Probably the same with the werelions."

"Any chance all of those alphas in one place will cause a problem?"

"Yes, a big one," Gordon said. "But most of them are sensible and don't want trouble. There are one or two who might decide to start a cock measuring exercise, but they're in the minority, and I'm hoping the others will calm anything before it gets out of hand."

"There was an argument brewing in the dining hall," I said. "It's why I left."

Gordon nodded. "The bride's father and the uncle of the groom, I assume," he said with a long sigh. "Both arseholes, I'm afraid. Thankfully, their kids are smarter than them, but they both adhere to the old idea that any slight, imagined or otherwise, must be met with aggression. Matthew can't stand either of them, so I'm guessing by the time we're done, at least one of them is going to get hurt."

"By Matthew?"

Gordon laughed. "No, not unless they try something with him, and that's why Tommy and you guys are here. We both know Tommy is one of the most powerful werewolves in any realm. Everyone respects him because he's earned it. And Diana? Everyone fears her."

"Because they've met her," I said, making Gordon laugh

again. "She almost got hit by an apple earlier. Never seen so many people look like they were going to piss themselves."

"Diana might actually be the scariest person I've ever met," Gordon said.

"I'm pretty sure that's why Tommy asked her to come along," I said. "That, and for Remy's amusement."

"Some of the weres don't know what to make of him," Gordon told me.

"They should be wary of him," I said. "He's small, got a big mouth, and is more than happy to back it up."

"How many more of his people did Tommy bring?"

"Twenty-six," I said. "Most of them are in the village getting a feel of the land, talking to the people who work here. This realm has a big security force, so they're trying not to step on any toes, but werewolves and werelions together is not exactly a recipe for a happy time."

"It's all very Shakespearian," Gordon said.

"Remy said the same thing," I told him with a chuckle. "Hopefully, it's less Romeo and Juliet, or Macbeth, and more…" I tried to think of a Shakespearian play that fit the bill. "A Midsummer Night's Dream."

"I'm not entirely sure that any of his plays would make for a fun thing to live through," Gordon said.

"Yeah, I was kind of grasping at straws there," I admitted. "Still, if no one dies, I'll consider this weekend a success."

"How about the loss of a few limbs?" Gordon asked.

I was about to reply when a figure burst out of the forest. He was naked from the waist up, wearing only a pair of denim, knee-length shorts that wouldn't have looked out of place on the Hulk after he'd turned back into Banner. Matthew was a muscular, hairy man which, seeing how he was a werewolf, wasn't exactly unusual, although he had several dozen scars over his body that he'd gotten before his change. The life of a Knight's Templar had been a hard one for many reasons, most of which Matthew didn't want to talk about.

"Nate," Matthew said, walking over and hugging me.

"You smell like pine needles," I told him.

"I've had an invigorating run," he said as Gordon passed him a red hair tie. Matthew cinched his long, dark hair before kissing his husband on the lips. "I missed you."

"It's been an hour," Gordon said with a wry smile.

Matthew's grin was full of warmth. "Even so, a run with my husband at my side is always preferable to one without."

"Go shower," Gordon said. "You really do smell like pine needles."

Matthew took a deep breath. "I smell of manly smells," he said, which caused Gordon to laugh.

I smiled; it was nice to see them both happy.

"You see how I am treated?" Matthew asked me. "An alpha, and my own husband mocks me."

"Would you prefer if I got someone else to mock you?" Gordon asked.

"Remy isn't busy," I said.

Matthew's eyes narrowed as he looked between us before a deep rumble of laughter burst from him. "I will go shower and change. Can I assume the wedding parties are still at one another's throats?"

I nodded. "I think some of the guests went to explore the realm instead, but basically, yes. It's going to be a long weekend."

Matthew sighed. "I was hoping they would be able to act

as adults for a few days."

"To be fair, it was only two of them when I left, although someone came in at the last minute and started shouting at everyone."

"Ah, that would probably be Sven, one of the werelion alphas," Gordon said. "Sven is not known for suffering fools gladly, and he's more interested in keeping the peace than he is in getting into petty squabbles."

"I don't think I've met him," I said.

"He's a good man," Matthew said, which was high praise from a werewolf. "I'm pretty sure Sven and his council are the reason the werelions and wolves haven't gone back to the old ways. He reminds me of Diana a lot. His presence here should stop anyone from thinking about acting in a stupid way."

"Is there a werewolf equivalent here?" I asked.

"The bride's mother, Victoria Walker," Gordon said. "She was one of those who left for a walk. She divorced the father some time ago, and she very much wears the alpha crown without contest. If she'd been there, no one would have started an argument. She'd have thrown them through the damn window."

"I haven't met her either," I said. "Haven't met the bride or groom for that matter."

"Beth and Logan," Gordon said. "Both are sweet kids, although they're about a century old, so the 'kids' thing is subjective. Beth is the spitting image of her mother, in both temperament and looks. Logan is a calm, relaxed, surfer dude type. I'm pretty certain there's never been a situation he couldn't charm himself out of. They're made for one another. A fact Beth's father and Logan's uncle both hate."

"That's why they were fighting," I said.

"Those two have been looking for a fight for a long time," Matthew said. "One killed someone the other liked, or some such. I don't even think either of them know anymore."

There was a shout from deeper in the forest, and all three of us turned to look in the direction.

"Did you see anyone else in there?" I asked Matthew, who shook his head.

I took a step toward the forest when a young woman with dark skin burst out of the dense woodland, stopping a few feet away. She was breathing heavily, her long dark hair sown with leaves. She was completely naked, her body covered in scratches. She looked up at us as if seeing us for the first time, horror in her face, and pitched forward onto the snow, a small crossbow bolt jutting between her shoulder blades.

"Oh shit," Gordon said as he rushed over to her.

"I'll get help," Matthew said, racing off.

I removed my coat and helped Gordon move the woman on to it.

"She's still breathing," Gordon said.

"You know her?" I asked.

Gordon nodded. "It's Victoria, the mother of the bride."

"Oh shit," I whispered as Victoria opened her eyes and screamed.

CHAPTER TWO

After Victoria screamed, a lot of things happened in a really short space of time. She passed out again, the crossbow bolt still lodged between her shoulder blades, and Gordon and me—with help from several of Tommy's people—carried her into the village, putting her in a medical facility that resembled a thatched cottage.

Tommy arrived with Diana, Remy, and half a dozen more of Tommy's people, and they took charge of the situation with all being sworn to secrecy until it could be ascertained what had happened.

I hung around just in case anyone decided they needed another shot at Victoria, while Tommy and his people went into the forest to search for the attacker, and hopefully figure out what the hell was going on.

I wasn't sure how long I remained outside the medical center, but it was long enough to notice the mood change in the workers of the realm. This wasn't the first time they'd had trouble, and from talking to a few of them, people often got drunk and stupid but it was the first time someone had tried to murder a guest.

An hour later, Tommy found me sat outside and handed me a new coat to keep me warm. "Any trouble?" he asked.

"Victoria is sedated, the bolt is out, and I have no idea what's happened since then," I told him. "We need to tell the people here. We need to tell her ex-husband and daughter. Sounds like she'll live, but no one can leave the castle."

Tommy nodded. "I'll take care of everything I can here, I'd like you to go down to the attack site. It's bad, Nate. Really, really bad."

"Worse than the mother of the bride being attacked?"

"There are three dead down there," Tommy whispered. "A groomsman, a bridesmaid, and one of Victoria's guards. They're... you need to go see before we start removing bodies. Gordon and Matthew are there with Diana and Remy, the latter are off hunting."

I got up and stretched. "How far away is it?"

"A mile, maybe a little more."

"Any way to get there quicker than running?"

"Not on foot, no," Tommy said. "There are tusked-horses in the stables, big shaggy things. They're pretty good at moving quickly but it's not a fun ride so I'm told."

"Why?"

"They move very fast and you just hold on for dear life."

I clapped my gloved hands together. "Sounds like fun." Tommy walked with me to the stables, and spoke to the hand working, who agreed to saddle up one of the animals for me.

"Tusked-horse," I said. "They couldn't have come up with a better name?"

"I suggested Tauntaun," Tommy said. "Apparently, that's copywritten and no one wanted to get sued."

"Of course you did," I said with a chuckle as the animal was brought out of the stables. It was at least a head higher than a warhorse, although slightly thinner. It had two, four-feet-long tusks that started at each side of its jaw—one of the tusks placed slightly higher than the other—but both looked like something you did not want to be on the end of. The horse was snowy white, with a shaggy, thick coat, and huge hooves.

"She's calm," the stable-hand said. "But not the fastest."

She looked down at me with dark eyes and moved her head so I could smooth my hand over her neck. "She's quite the stunner," I said before climbing into the saddle and getting comfortable. I patted the back of her neck as the stable-hand fed her an apple that was the size of my face.

"I don't know where I'm going," I told Tommy.

"There's only one trail, just follow it," he said.

"What's her name?" I asked the stable-hand.

"Sorcery."

"Oh, we're going to get along brilliantly," I said with a smile.

We trotted out of the village and across the moat, Tommy beside me. "Nate," he said when we were outside the village.

I stared down at my friend; he looked tired. "It's bad," I said. "I know."

"We need to get this sorted, quickly. Those arseholes in the castle just need an excuse to reignite a damn war between werelions and werewolves. We can't afford that."

"We'll figure it out," I said. "We were there when the peace was signed, we're not going to be there when it's broken."

Sorcery started off into the forest at what I considered a pleasant speed. She clearly knew the way along the winding path, but after a while the trees either side started to become denser, darker, as the canopy allowed less and less light into the forest. It wasn't long before I was in darkness, and Sorcery's speed picked up.

Within a few minutes we were hurtling along the path, with me holding on for dear life as Sorcery moved and darted between trees only she saw as we whizzed past. More than once, leaves and branches brushed my hair and face, but I kept as low as I could, and reminded myself that Tommy had to deal with the families, and that was much worse.

Eventually, the darkness began to dissipate as the branches above opened their arms, and Sorcery slowed to a trot.

"Good girl," I said, patting her neck. "Good, terrifying girl."

Sorcery walked up to two guards, both of whom nodded in my direction. One took the reins from me, and I climbed down off Sorcery.

"That took less than a few minutes," I said, looking back into the darkness behind me.

"The tusked-horses move like water," the guard with the reins said. "We'll take care of this one while you're working."

"Thanks," I said. "Her name is Sorcery. She likes apples."

I patted her on the neck again and thanked her, before walking along the pathway that looked like it had been carved out of the brambles and trees that crouched either side. I stepped under an archway of flowers and into a large clearing a few hundred feet in diameter and ringed with huge, dark trees. The ground was covered in snow, which was splattered red in patches.

"Nate," Gordon said as he peeled off a set of latex gloves and put them in a bag beside him. He was crouched next to the body of a naked man, and as I stood beside him, Gordon got to his feet with a loud sigh.

I nodded a greeting and looked around the clearing. There were two other naked bodies on the ground, both with members of Tommy's security team and, or, members of the medical staff in the village.

"Two men, one woman. Well, two women if you include Victoria," Gordon said. "All hit with arrows, but these three had their throats cut deep enough that they may as well have decapitated them and saved the effort."

"Not that I want to disparage how people spend their free time, but this was an orgy, yes?" I asked.

"I'm not sure it's an orgy with only four people," Remy said as he walked over to me, Diana at his side.

"I'll bow down to your knowledge on such things," I said.

"He's right," Diana said. "Orgies have more people. This was just four people fucking."

"Okay, semantics aside," I said, not wanting to get into a conversation about the technical parts of an orgy. "They were enjoying themselves and were attacked."

"The attackers had crossbows," Remy said. "At least two of them to kill four weres without any of them fighting back. One of the males, the werewolf, had four bolts in his body."

"Two werewolves, two werelions," Gordon said. "Before you ask."

"They were doing a lot for species relations," Remy said. "But there are a lot of questions we can't answer."

"Such as?" I asked.

"There are no tracks," Diana said. "Whoever did this, did it without leaving a trace. I think they used the trees; the trajectory of the bolts points to that being the case. I followed the scent into the forest and lost it about half a mile to the south, near some mountains."

"They came prepared to hunt people who could smell

them," I said.

Diana nodded. "Werewolves and werelions were the intended prey here. No idea why though."

"Victoria is lucky she's alive," I said.

Remy and Diana glanced at each other.

"You think she was involved?" I asked.

"I find it odd that three people died with multiple wounds, no tracks, and scents that vanish," Diana said. "But they let Victoria go."

"She could have been lucky," I said.

"And I could have been Brad Pitt, but I'm not," Remy said.

"What?"

Remy shrugged. "Made sense in my head."

"He's had a long day," Diana said with a shake of her head. "Nate, these people came to kill. Victoria would have to be the luckiest person alive, or they let her live."

"She's either involved, or she's the message," I said.

Diana nodded. "But she passed out before she could give it."

"Great," I said with a sigh. "Do we know their names?"

"The guard's name is Kozma Imre," Diana said. "He's a Hungarian who has worked for Victoria for many years."

"The other two?" I asked.

"Mona Reece," Remy said. "And Varol Musat. She was from Wales, and he was from Romania. We're looking into their pasts right now, but early suggestions are they're both clean."

"You want it to get worse?" Gordon asked, passing me one of the crossbow bolts, the tip of which was gone

"Not silver," I said, surprised. "Who comes to kill weres and doesn't bring the one thing that kills them?"

"It's a basilisk-tooth blade," Gordon said. "The tips vanish with a killing shot. Victoria is more than a little lucky."

"These are rare, expensive," I said, turning the bolt over in my hands. "And more than that, there's no way you'd take a bolt to the back to try and show you were the innocent party when you're involved. She'd have to be insane."

"So, she's the message," Remy said. "We just need to figure out what that message is."

"The groomsman, bridesmaid, and a guard were all involved along with the mother of the bride," I said, more to myself than anyone else. "Any of them have a relationship outside of getting their freak on in the forest?"

"We'll check," Diana said.

"I'll be especially tactful," Remy said.

I stared at Remy for a heartbeat, before looking at Diana. "Don't let Remy ask anyone if they knew Victoria liked to fuck people in the woods."

"But that was my opening question," Remy said, throwing his hands in the air in mock indignation.

"He'll behave," Diana said, her tone suggesting that Remy wouldn't have a choice.

Remy smiled, but it vanished when he looked over at the dead bridesmaid. "Nate, whoever did this needs to suffer for it. The bolt would have killed them, or at the very least paralyzed them while they had their necks slit to the bone. This was an assassination."

I nodded. "Agreed. So which one were they assassinating?"

"We'll look into all three of them," Diana said. "You going hunting?"

I nodded. "Where's Matthew?"

"He's out there," Gordon said. "He found a bolt on the ground to the east."

"They split up after the kill," I said. "I'll go find him."

"Nate, be careful," Remy said, suddenly serious. "You get hit with one of these things, and you could die."

The was a loud rustle at one end of the clearing and several of the guards drew swords as Matthew emerged from the dense foliage, chest heaving.

"I ran for miles," Matthew said. "Nothing. I'm going back to the castle to talk to Tommy and try to figure out how we get on top of this."

I walked around the clearing, looking at each of the three bodies in turn as Matthew, Diana, and Remy exited the clearing. Each body had the same wounds, although the male werewolf had been hit with more arrows than the others, and the female werelion had two more stab wounds in the chest.

"There's no passion in the kill, no loss of control, I don't think this was personal," I muttered, not realizing that Gordon was beside me.

"You agree this was an assassination?" Gordon asked as the female werelion was placed in a body bag.

I nodded. "But why leave Victoria alive? She's the most influential of all three. Which makes me think one of these three was the intended target, maybe more than one. Someone paid to have at least one of them killed."

"Maybe the hiring was personal," Gordon suggested.

I nodded again. "These were clinical kills," I said pointing to the bodies. "The guard at the very least was a trained professional. I can't imagine someone with Victoria's influence having a newbie protecting her. None of them fought back. Even when you consider all were having sex at the time, none of them did anything but die, except Victoria. If the assassins were hired, they didn't come cheap. And they knew these four would come here for sex."

I spent some time walking around the forest close to the clearing, using my fire magic to change my vision to thermal and checking for tracks. The trees had some remnants high up in the branches, but the continued freezing temperatures made them fade quickly. I was just as likely to track an animal as I was a person, and I didn't know the realm well enough to go traipsing through the wilderness only to get lost.

I emerged from the tree line back into the clearing and found Tommy waiting.

"You find anything?" I asked.

Tommy shook his head. "Victoria is asleep. She'll be okay, but they had to sedate her. The basilisk-tooth-blade tip was still intact, but it was seemingly coated with some kind of paralyzing agent. It was all around the edge of the wound. On the end of the arrow shaft too. It's incredible she managed to run feet, let alone over a mile."

"She must be a strong woman," I said.

"She's certainly that," Tommy agreed. "We had to tell the wedding parties. The reactions ranged from out and out anger, to crying, to in one particular unpleasant case, laughing. That was the groom's uncle."

"The dickhead in the dining hall?"

Tommy nodded. "The one and the same. Victoria wasn't always well liked, but she was respected, and feared."

"She wasn't the target," I said. "I don't think so anyway.

If she was, they did a shitty job, and nothing about this looks like the work of amateurs."

"It was well known Victoria was sleeping with one of her guards," Tommy said. "It wasn't well known that she was sleeping with a groomsman and bridesmaid."

"Did people know those two were in a relationship, or just shagging?"

Tommy shook his head. "No, although I spoke to the bride and her other bridesmaids, and all of them said that Mona had been happy with a new man. She hadn't told anyone about him other than to say he wasn't human. Mona told them she'd reveal all after the wedding."

"And the groom and his groomsmen?" I asked.

"Varol was well liked, and a similar story to Mona. New, secretive girlfriend everyone wanted to know more about, but he told them it was new, and he didn't want to scare her off."

"So, we have three bodies, all of them appear to be well liked, two of them were secretly dating, and all of them were shagging in the freezing cold forest. I assume they didn't get seen in the castle."

"That's a good assumption, but we need to look into it more," Tommy said. "I also want to know how these assassins got in and out of this realm. There's meant to be only one realm gate, and that's guarded."

"So there's either a second gate, or they came through with the wedding guests."

"Or workers."

"You know that time I said yes to helping you?" I said with a long sigh. "I'm regretting it."

"Liar," Tommy said with a smile, rubbing his hand across his bushy beard. "You wanted to keep busy, and this is going to do that."

"You getting Olivia in to help?" I asked.

"No, this is a neutral realm, so Avalon's influence is probably going to be even less than mine. Besides, if you think people on the Earth Realm don't trust Avalon, those who live here all year 'round pretty much moved here to get away from Avalon in its entirety."

"I'm not exactly shocked," I said. "So, how do you want to play this?" The three bodies had all been removed now, but there were still members of Tommy's security team going through the clearing, looking for anything that might help.

"We can't track them through the wilderness," Tommy said. "If Diana lost their scent, then no one else is going to pick it up again. We go back to the castle and try to figure out who wants who dead."

"They're a bunch of werewolves and werelions," I said. "They all want each other dead."

"I never said this was going to be easy," Tommy admitted.

"Come help me for the weekend," I quoted. "It'll be easy, it'll be fun. You'll enjoy yourself."

"I find it distasteful that you'd use my own words against me at this time," Tommy said. "It's not like I could have foreseen this."

I stared at Tommy for a few seconds.

"Okay, yeah, something was going to happen," Tommy admitted. "We just need to stop more somethings from happening next."

"I want the families separated," I said. "There are a few hundred guests, and there's no way everything that happened here can be kept secret. Someone knows something, and once one person knows, it's pretty likely more than one person will know soon after."

"Only dead people keep secrets," Tommy said.

I looked back at the blood-stained snow. "Get a necromancer here too. The dead need to give up what they know."

CHAPTER THREE

After returning Sorcery to the stables, Tommy and I headed to the village to find that Victoria had woken. She was still groggy and barely capable of putting together a coherent sentence.

"It's going to be a while before you can talk to her," Gordon told us as I spotted Diana and Remy strolling over with Sky.

I was glad to see Sky; the adopted daughter of Hades and Persephone was one of my closest friends. Centuries earlier, her Native American father and white mother had been murdered when she was only a child, and she'd been raised by two of the most powerful beings in any realm.

Sky's dark grey suit matched the leather bag she passed to one of the people who worked in the realm, and they hurried off to take it to her room. "I hear you've got some dead people problems," she said after hugging me, and fist bumping Tommy.

"Did you tell her?" Tommy asked Diana and Remy.

"We told her everything," Diana said.

"It's a good job you were coming anyway," I said.

"I'm just sorry I couldn't have been here earlier," Sky said. "So, where are the dead?"

"Nate, you want to go with Sky?" Tommy said. "I need to go talk to the guests and workers, try to figure out a way to stop anyone deciding to use this as an excuse to pick a fight."

As I walked through the village with Diana, Remy, and Sky, there was a noticeable change in tone from those who worked in the realm all year around; a fear not just about what had happened, but what might happen next. There was an air of trying to look like it was business as usual when it was anything but.

We stopped outside a small hut where two of Tommy's security people stood guard. "This is a morgue?" I asked, looking around. It was some distance from anything residential, but it appeared to be just another thatched hut in a village of similar thatched huts.

"Most of anything not looking authentic is underground," Diana said.

"Don't want to spoil the illusion of the time," Remy said, rolling his eyes. "It's not like vast people died back in the Middle Ages or anything."

"The sanitized version of the Middle Ages," Sky said. "Murder isn't meant to exist here. I think that's why people are freaking out. They've gotten used to being in their safe bubble, and now it's gone. They have to confront the fact there's a murderer here, at least one."

"To be fair, it's never a good time to confront that fact," Remy said, the guards nodding to us when we stepped inside the almost empty hut.

The only thing inside was a door, which had runes carved into the dark wood that burned yellow and would occasionally pulse with weak light.

Diana touched one of the runes, and the door slid back to reveal a dimly lit set of stairs that led underground.

As creepy as those stairs were, we had all been in considerably worse situations than some badly lit steps, and descended them without comment, reaching a large open reception area shortly after.

"This way," Diana said, leading us along what could have been any hospital in any part of the Earth Realm. I spotted a map, which showed the structure to be a giant circle that ran beneath the village. It was divided into four parts; each one used for something different. The medical quarter had four floors, and from the looks of things, was barely used.

On our way to the morgue, we passed three members of staff, all wearing medical ID tags.

Unsurprisingly, the morgue looked pretty much like every morgue I'd ever visited.

Diana went to the cold chamber and opened one of the drawers, sliding free one of the victims—the guard—before repeating the process twice more.

Sky walked the line of bodies. "So, you want me to see if I can pick anything up from their spirits?"

"If you think that would work," Diana said.

"It'll work," Sky said. "It just depends on how traumatic the death was. Memories in spirits start to dissipate pretty quickly, but I might be able to get something. It's going to take a while though, depending on what I find and what I have to work with."

"Take as long as you need," I said.

I caught Remy staring at the wounds on the guard.

"You okay?" I asked him.

"This guy got shot with four basilisk-tooth-tipped arrows," he said. "I'd have thought one was enough. They're not cheap, and using four to kill someone is like trying to kill a wasp with an AK-47."

"Anyone else concerned that Remy has a point?" Diana asked.

"Also, why slit the throats after?" Remy continued, flipping Diana off without looking her way, which earned him a chuckle from her.

"Overkill," I said.

"We'll soon find out," Sky said, taking a metal stool and placing it beside the body of the young woman. "Sorry, kid," she said softly, and a second later her head dipped forward.

"You two go back," I said. "I'll keep Sky company."

"You sure?" Remy asked. "Victoria is surrounded by heavily-armed bastards. It's just you in here."

"Oh, I'm sorry, Remy," I said. "We must have just met. I'm Nate Garrett, I can create lightning and throw it at people."

"Why don't you want to go back?" Diana asked Remy, suddenly serious.

"Victoria is protected by a lot of people," Remy said. "Tommy is busy and has a lot of protection, but if someone discovered that we had a necromancer who could talk to spirits and tell you what happened, who do you think they'd go after first?"

The lights shut off, flicking back on to dim emergency lighting a second later.

"Okay, Remy, you need to stop being right," Diana said.

"It's pretty off-putting," I told him.

"It's freaking me out too, guys," Remy said, drawing a sword from the sheath at his hip. "Any chance this is just a power surge or something?"

"No," Diana and I said in unison.

"Remy, stay here, keep Sky safe," I told him. "Diana, we

need to patrol the corridor outside. You go left, I'll go right, and we'll hit the end of this quarter and double-back to here. No need to check other floors. If you find someone who doesn't want to play nice, try not to kill them before we find out what's going on."

"No promises," Diana told me.

Diana set off and I followed soon after, leaving Sky under Remy's protection. I knew he would give his lives to do so, and anyone who underestimated Remy in a fight usually ended up with a dagger in their throat.

I set off along the corridor, and had only made it a few feet when the already dim lighting began to flicker again, this time turning red. I could still see, but now shadows cast an other-worldly appearance to them. Every time I walked past an open door, or there was a turn in the hallway, I had to stop and check to make sure I was alone.

Somewhere in the distance of the hallway there were noises of things being dropped, the scrape of items being dragged along the wall and floor. Someone was trying to scare me, which probably wasn't the best use of their time, but I figured they thought I'd drop my guard and they could come running in and kill me without any problems.

I'd made it all the way back to the reception area when I found who I assumed to be the cause of the noises. A figure dressed all in dark colors rolled his considerably large shoulders, and drew a short sword; its slightly curved blade took my attention immediately.

"A basilisk-tooth blade," I said. "I don't know who's paying you, but they're certainly paying a lot. Those things are rare."

"You were not part of the payment," the man said, his voice muffled by his hooded mask. "Let me do what I came to do, and I will let you go."

"No," I said. "You won't."

"No," the man said with a chuckle. "But you'd be surprised how many people believe I would."

"You're a dick."

The man positioned himself into a fighting stance, the blade down by his leg, ready to whip up at me in a moment's notice. He clearly hadn't considered me much of a threat.

"How about you tell me who paid for the murders, and I'll let you go," I said. "Or at least I'll let you have a head start."

"You will regret coming here today," the man said, lowering his stance.

I sighed. "I already do."

He sprang at me, flicking the sword up toward my chest in a move that was so obvious, I was a little insulted he'd used it.

I blasted him in the chest with a plume of air, sending him spiraling back across the reception area.

"Wanna try again?" I asked him.

"You're a sorcerer," he said, getting back to his feet, the irritation in his voice easy to hear.

"You're quick," I said. "I can see why you were hired."

"Magical attacks won't work on me," he said, and I noticed the white runes on his dark armor had lit up.

"Rune-scribed armor," I said. "Basilisk-tooth blades, and I assume an assortment of other talents. Someone wanted to make sure the job went to the best."

He sprinted toward me again; threw something from his hip. I created a shield of air around me, and the half-dozen marble sized spheres impacted without causing me any issues.

"You'll have to do better than—" The half a dozen spheres exploded, throwing a cloud of darkness all around me.

I darted back, putting distance between myself and the cloud that impeded my vision, throwing up another shield of air. The second my magic touched the particles of smoke, they exploded, throwing me back down the hall. I was uninjured, although my pride had certainly taken a battering.

The assassin was on me in a second, swiping at my head as I rolled back to my feet. I grabbed his arm as I stood, and turned into him, throwing him over my shoulder and onto the hard floor. He landed and rolled right back to his feet as if nothing had happened.

We faced off, glaring at one another. I was beginning to regret the idea of needing any assailants alive. It was becoming more work than I'd wanted.

He dashed forward, the blade coming up from his hip again, before he turned it and thrust it forward, trying to catch me off balance as I moved back. I stepped to his side, and threw a ball of fire behind me, right into the cloud, which ignited. White glyphs lit up over the backs of my hands as I wrapped myself in air magic as the explosion tore through the reception area, throwing me aside. The would-be assassin hurtled past, smashing through the closed door of a nearby room.

"Bet that hurt," I said to myself as I got to my feet. Most of the cloud had dissipated, although I wasn't certain that using my magic again wouldn't result in another explosion.

I stepped inside the hospital room to find the assassin wobbling on his feet, holding onto the bed as he tried to remain upright.

"You don't look so good," I told him and punched him in the side of the head. He dropped to his knees and I slammed his head against the metal rail of the bed.

His blade was on the ground close to the bed, so I picked it up, turning it over in my hand to examine the craftsmanship.

It wasn't particularly well made, it wasn't elegant, but then it didn't need to be. It just needed to be stabby.

The assassin made a gurgling sound, presumably because I'd shattered his nose earlier. I grabbed his hooded mask and pulled it free, revealing a mass of blood and scar tissue beneath.

"I know this might seem rude, but what happened to you?" I asked, tossing the mask aside.

He spat blood onto the tiled floor. "You have no idea what is going to happen to you," he said. "No idea."

I sensed movement behind me, spun to the side, just in time to avoid a second assassin lunging at me with their own basilisk-tooth blade. I parried the strike and stepped back as far as I could from the two assassins, even though the injured one remained on his knees.

"Bad news, guys," I said. "There's two of you."

"And only one of you," the man on the floor said.

"Yes," I nodded slightly. "It's just not your day."

The still masked assassin darted forward. I parried, stepping to his side, and slammed the blade up under his ribs. "I only need one of you," I said, pushing him aside.

The assassin on his knees sprung toward me, a normal dagger in his hand. I kept back as his comrade's body fell to the floor, and the injured assassin used that opportunity to almost dive over the body. I blasted him in the chest with my air magic, which threw him back across the room. The dagger dropped from his fingers, and a whip of my air magic sent it under the bed, out of the assassin's reach.

"I don't think you understand the predicament you're in," I said. "You're going to answer my questions, one way or another."

There was a roar outside the room, and I left the injured

assassin alone for a moment, stepping into the hallway to see Diana tackle a fleeing assassin to the ground, where she head butted him over and over as she turned into her werebear form. Diana in full werebear form was massive and terrifying, a nightmare version of a grizzly bear.

"We've got one in there," I told her, pointing to the hospital room.

Diana looked up at me and tore the assassins head clean off his shoulders, throwing it aside with a shrug as the assassin I'd left inside the room sprinted past me. I tripped him with a tendril of air, sending him headfirst into the reception area desk.

"He looks hurt," Diana said.

"You have no idea how much more work it was keeping him alive," I told her as the assassin crawled across the floor, leaving a trail of blood along the reception desk as he used it for leverage.

Diana walked over to the assassin and placed a massive paw on his back, pinning him in place.

"I'd stop struggling," I told him as I crouched beside his head. "Now, is there something you'd like to tell us?"

He laughed. "Goodbye, little sorcerer."

I wasn't entirely sure how to respond to that, and was even less so when he melted, causing Diana to jump back.

Diana and I shared an expression of confusion.

"Any ideas?" I asked.

Diana shook her head. "It's not brilliant."

Several taps sounded from the other side of the reception area, and I watched as half a dozen of the marble sized items rolled along the floor before detonating.

A massive plume of smoke was thrown up all around the

reception area, and quickly expanded to cover both myself and Diana. Half a dozen dark-clad assassins ran out of the corridor after the explosion.

"So, they were just hiding there?" I asked, noticing that only one of them had a basilisk-tooth blade.

"Something feel off to you?" Diana asked as the assassins charged.

She plowed into them, throwing two aside with one swipe of her enormous paw. I avoided the thrust of a basilisk-tooth blade, stepped into his guard and drove my elbow into his throat. I grabbed the blade, broke his wrist, and stabbed him in the head, pushing him aside as a second assassin took his place.

I'd killed four, but they just kept coming. "Diana, you got this?"

Diana tore the head from another assassin and threw it at one of his companions. "I'm good," she said.

I ran past the battle to find another assassin charging down the corridor toward me. He lunged at me with a dagger, which I removed from him then stabbed him in the ribs with it before unleashing a torrent of lighting into the blade, which cooked him from the inside out. The smoking husk of his body fell to the ground, and I continued on.

The last door on the corridor was open, and the sounds of heavy breathing were easy to hear. I stepped inside, saw an un-masked man—whose face was similarly scarred as the one I'd seen earlier—and punched him in the face with an air-magic-wrapped fist. He collapsed to the ground, unconscious.

I poked my head back out of the door. "You okay down there?" I shouted into the eerie silence of the corridor.

"What the hell just happened?" Diana shouted back. "Everyone turned to mush."

I looked back at the man on the ground, he was breathing, but he was sweaty and appeared as though he'd run miles.

Diana appeared in the doorway behind me. "Sorcerer?"

I nodded. "Probably." I moved him into a sitting position at the far end of the room and waited for him to wake.

He went from groggy to utterly terrified in a few seconds as his new predicament dawned on him.

Diana cleared her throat, and the man's eyes snapped to her. "If you send any more of your clones in here, I'm going to rip your legs off and beat you to death with them."

"And she'll do it too," I told him. "I just saw her crush one of the heads of a clone like it was a grape."

The man looked between me and Diana, and when she smiled, I got the impression that any level of fight the man had left, just vanished.

"If I tell you, you have to keep me safe," he said softly.

I nodded.

"No," he said. "No, no I didn't!"

"Didn't what?" Diana asked.

The man's head exploded, and I put up a hasty shield of air to stop us from being covered in bits of gore.

Diana sighed. "Now that's new."

I nodded and wondered if it was too late to tell Tommy I didn't want to help. "Yeah, this whole thing is just getting weirder and weirder."

CHAPTER FOUR

"So, his head just...exploded?" Remy asked as Diana carried the body of the decapitated assassin into the morgue.

"Yes," Diana said, dropping said body onto a metal gurney.

"Why is Diana covered in more blood than you?" Remy asked.

"I rip and tear," Diana said by way of explanation. "And now I need to shower and scrub." She left the morgue without another word, stepping aside to allow Gordon and Matthew entry.

I'd contacted them as well as Tommy as soon as the assassin's head had detonated, and laid out the whole sorry tale. I wasn't sure how the assassin's head had blown up, or even why, but I was pretty sure it wasn't good news. Tommy had asked if I could pry myself away from dead people to come help him deal with the mass of wedding guests. Apparently, they were starting to become an irritant, and Tommy's tone suggested he was fairly close to picking one of them up to throw at another. I told him I'd be there as soon as I checked on Sky.

"How is she?" Gordon asked, nodding toward Sky, who sat at the far end of the room, her eyes closed.

"I need wine," she said without opening them. "I assume you'd like me to go through the spirit of that assassin too?"

"If you can," I said.

"You know, it would be great if the next time someone dies, you can make sure they do so fighting," Sky said, opening her eyes and getting to her feet. "This sucks."

Gordon, Matthew, and I left the morgue with Remy a few moments later.

"Tommy asked me to come down and check the bodies out," Gordon said. "He wanted to be able to tell both parties that someone outside of his security people had a look. I think the werelions and werewolves both think the other side is betraying them."

"Even though both sides lost people?" Remy asked.

"It helps if you realize that both sides are also idiots," Matthew said, his tone suggesting he was very much done dealing with all involved.

"That why you accompanied Gordon?" Remy asked. "Are you hiding?"

"Yes," Matthew said without pause. "Also, because he's my husband and I love him."

"Good save," Gordon said with a slight smile.

"Wait," Remy said. "Why aren't the werelions getting someone they trust to be involved?"

"They have someone working with Tommy," Matthew said. "Two of them, to be precise."

"Because there are two of you," I said.

"Pretty much," Matthew said and rubbed his eyes. "It's stupid politics and petty grievances getting in the way of safety and getting things done. The uncle of the groom and his sister."

"The shouty man from the dinner?" Remy said. "Oh joy."

"Yeah, he's a dick," Gordon said. "His name is Viktor Elkund. His sister is Alexandra Lindahl. Different fathers. Their mother was a werelion."

"Viktor, the one who laughed when he was told about Victoria being hurt?" I asked.

"That would be the one," Gordon said.

"I know Viktor is a loudmouth, but what is Alexandra like?" I asked.

"Alexandra likes to go by Lex," Matthew said. "She was the wife of a Viking chief, and rumor has it she was the reason he stayed chief for as long as he did. She's very much the smarts of the family. She's got a viscous streak in her too. So does Viktor for that matter."

"Are they people you can work with?" I asked.

"Lex, yes," Gordon said. "We've been working with her to foster closer relations between her pride in the Nordic countries. And yes, I did say countries. She has a pride of nearly a hundred lions at this point, which is all but unheard of. Makes hers one of the largest in the world, probably the largest in Western Europe. Viktor has his own pride too; they operate out of Eastern Europe. No one is quite sure of the numbers, but they certainly have Romania, Slovakia, and Hungary all in their group. Last we heard they wanted to move into Russia, but there's already at least half a dozen prides there, and they do not play well with others."

"He's trying to out-do his sister?" I asked.

"If you ask me in an official capacity as the alpha of a werewolf pack, I would say no, of course not," Matthew said without emotion.

"And if I asked you as a friend?" I asked.

"Fuck yes, he's a hundred percent pissed off that his sister is doing better," Matthew said.

"Also, allegedly, his sister is fucking his wife on the side," Gordon said. "Allegedly."

"Ah, the old finger air quotes," Remy said. "Quick question, is Viktor's wife at the wedding? Just curious if there will be some comedy gold at some point."

"Yes," Matthew said. "She wasn't at the meal."

"And neither was Lex," Gordon said.

"He's enjoying this," I said to Matthew, nodding toward Gordon.

"Gordon does not like Viktor," Matthew said. "Do you, my love?"

"He's an arsehole," Gordon said. "A bully, a thug, a mean son of a bitch. His own brother, the father of the groom, hates his guts, and his own wife refused to stay in the same house as him. Everyone hates Viktor except the people he's giving power to. They love the nasty little prick."

"You really hate him," Remy said. "What did he do?"

Gordon looked at the ground for a second. "He murdered a friend of mine. A century ago. She was with her husband, a human, in Bucharest. She was a werewolf. She did not take kindly to Viktor's attempt to... let's say woo her. Her husband stepped in. Viktor had them both murdered. From what I hear, he had the husband hunted through the forest and slaughtered like a..." he paused and looked at Remy.

"Like a fox in a hunt?" Remy asked, his voice taking on a hard tone.

Gordon nodded.

Remy turned to me. "I think I want to stab Viktor in the

testicles. Repeatedly."

"Their bodies were found nailed to trees near a were-wolf pack," Gordon said. "No one was charged. No one was punished. There was no evidence that it was him, but one of the were-lions who was with him on the hunt confessed it to me."

"A dying confession?" I asked.

"Yes," Gordon said.

I didn't need to know more. "Okay, I'll keep an eye on Viktor. If he needs putting down, what happens to the truce?"

"If you kill someone, probably nothing," Matthew said. "You're not a were of any kind, you'd be seen as carrying out a fair punishment—so long as it was warranted. If one of us did it, or one of them to a wolf. There would be problems."

"So, if a wolf is involved, it needs to be a wolf or not a were doing the justice, same for a lion?"

Matthew and Gordon nodded.

"Just once I'd like to be involved with the world of weres that doesn't need me..." I paused. "Actually, screw it, just that doesn't involve me at all. Every time I get involved; it always becomes much more complicated because of politics."

"Welcome to our lives," Gordon said. "Happy to have you on board."

"Any update on Victoria?" I asked.

"She was just coming out of it when we came down here," Gordon said. "Even for someone as powerful as her, she's still more than a little out of it. I don't know what was in the basilisk-tooth blade to make her have that reaction, but it was bad."

"Any idea what the poison was?" I asked.

"Manticore venom," Gordon said.

"Wait, they were using manticore venom and basilisk-tooth blades?" Remy asked. "What's the point?"

"What do you mean?" Matthew asked.

"Well, basilisk-tooth blades kill you, right?" Remy asked. "And manticore venom is a paralyzing agent. Why coat the weapon that kills you in something designed not to?"

"Remy really needs to stop making sense," Gordon said.

"Something isn't right here," I said.

"That was not a fun experience," Sky said as the door opened and she stepped out, looking a little wobbly. "We need to talk." She pointed at me. "That sucked ass."

"You okay?" I asked her, moving my hands just in case I needed to catch her.

"That last one," she said waving her hands about. "Well, he had some kind of really fucked-up life. It took a lot out of me. I'm feeling a little sleepy now."

"And the first three?" Remy asked.

"The basilisk-tooth blade did something to their heads when they died," Sky said, wobbling from side to side. "They didn't see a damn thing. The assassin couldn't remember what his employer looked like; it was scrubbed out of his head. Could have been a pink elephant for all I know."

"Are there wereelephants?" Remy asked.

"No," Gordon and Matthew said in unison.

"Just checking," Remy said, muttering wereelephant under his breath a few more times. "Funny word."

"We'll look around down here," Matthew said. "Take Sky outside for some fresh air."

"That," Sky said, gesticulating to the ceiling. "Is a fucking wonderful idea." She stepped up to Remy. "I like you, little fox."

"Is this what drunk Sky is like?" Remy asked me. "Because drunk Sky rocks."

"Son of a bitch had something in his head," Sky said to me, whispering the last word and tapping herself on the head. "Head." She giggled.

"I've never once heard Sky giggle," Remy said.

"Let's get her outside," I said as Sky's behavior appeared to be getting worse.

"Nate," Sky said as we started up the stairs to the hut above. "Whoever did this, is not a good person."

"Yeah, I know," I said, throwing her arm around my shoulder and helping her up the stairs.

"Telepath," she said. "Tele...eeeee... path."

We'd reached the top of the stairs and Remy and I managed to get Sky outside. The fresh air hit her, and we walked ten paces, before she turned and vomited.

"I'll find her some water," Remy said, genuine concern in his voice.

"She okay?" One of the village regulars, a young man with a round face asked.

"She'll be okay." I hoped. "I'm sorry about your hut."

"She's not the first and won't be the last," he said.

"I bet she's the first to do it after going into the spirit of an assassin," I told him.

Remy returned with the water, and Sky washed out her mouth before taking small sips.

"I'm good," she said, settling herself on the ground.

"You sure?" Remy asked.

Sky patted him on the head again. "Thank you, little

fox."

Remy smiled. "Any time."

Sky smiled back. "Nate, a telepath put all kind of horrible stuff inside that assassin's brain, it bled into his spirit. It was like drinking a gallon of vodka after not eating anything for a week. His spirit was like wading through sludge."

"You sure you're okay?"

Sky nodded. "I'm going to just stay here for a bit. I'll catch you up and tell you everything when my brain isn't spinning, and it's had time to sort out what I actually discovered. Right now, it's just a jumbled mess of stuff."

"I'll stay with her," Remy said.

"Thank you," Sky said as Remy sat beside her, his sheathed sword across his lap.

"I just think drunk Sky is funny," Remy said dismissively, although we all knew that for all his joking, he would stand by any of our sides should we need it.

"Nate," Sky said after I'd taken a few steps away. I turned back to her. "Whoever did this is evil," she said. "Not a bit unpleasant, but evil. Fucking with a person's spirit like that, twisting it so that when they die they can't know peace? That's a whole new level of messed up. Be careful."

"Always," I told her. "Come find me when you can walk without the world spinning."

Sky closed her eyes, and slumped to the side, resting her head against Remy's shoulder.

CHAPTER FIVE

I found Tommy in the courtyard of the castle, standing on top of a raised platform that hadn't been there earlier. There was half a dozen of his people there too. Added to that, were fifty people all talking at once.

"Enough," Tommy said, his voice snapping across everyone. "I'm trying to tell you what's going on."

"Can't trust a werewolf," one of the crowd shouted.

"He's working for them," another continued.

"You all agreed to hire me to do security," Tommy said, clearly exasperated.

"Enough," I shouted, using my air magic to raise the word by enough decibels that it reverberated around the courtyard.

Everyone turned to look at me.

"Some of you know who I am," I said. "Some of you will know that Tommy brought me here because I don't give two shits about your petty, centuries-old nonsense. I don't care whose grandfather fucked whose grandmother. I don't care who killed who, or who tried to kill who, but if any of you accuse Tommy of doing anything but his best for you, I will personally eject you from the highest rampart of this castle like a goddamned missile." A whip of fire trailed from my hand, touching the cobbled stone, causing steam to rise all around me.

No one spoke for several seconds.

"Go back to your rooms," Tommy said. "We will talk to each of you in turn."

"Oh, one more thing," I said. "If any of you hired the son of a bitch that tried to murder me and my friends, we're going to have problems. I would consider handing yourself in now, because I am not in the mood to hunt for you."

Shockingly, no one raised their hands to confess, but I figured I might as well try.

When the courtyard was clear—except for Tommy and me—he sat down on the makeshift platform.

"Victoria was poisoned with manticore venom," I said as I sat beside him. "And we had an assassin whose head exploded. Sky will tell me more when she doesn't want to throw up her own lungs."

"Everyone is having a particularly shit day," Tommy said.

"Except the assassin behind it all," I said. "They're on form."

"I'm beginning to regret agreeing to this job," Tommy said.

"If it helps, I very much regret saying yes."

Tommy laughed. "Thanks for your support."

"Any time, my friend," I told him, giving him a thumbs up. "So, Viktor and Lex, they around?"

"The werelion contingent?" Tommy said. "Lex is useful, but I'd rather have a rabid bat helping out than Viktor."

I spotted a man and woman stood in the doorway to the castle, they were watching us with interest.

"Beth and Logan," Tommy said. "I get the feeling they want to talk to us."

"We don't bite," I called out.

Beth was a few inches over five feet, with long red hair and dark skin. The man was taller by at least a foot, with shaggy blonde hair that really did look like it belonged to the typical surfer dude image. Both looked concerned as they walked over to us hand-in-hand.

"Tommy," Logan said, shaking his hand. "Thank you so much for being here."

"You hired me to run security," Tommy said. "I expected drunken stupidity, maybe a few brawls, but I hadn't counted on assassins, got to be honest."

"Varol and Mona were our friends," Logan said. "And my mother-in-law was attacked, her guard murdered. No one expected any of this."

"We want to help however we can," Beth said. "Do we need to postpone the wedding?"

Tommy shook his head. "Maybe that's what the killers want. Maybe that makes things worse. We don't know yet. We need more intel. We need Victoria awake and talking."

Beth turned to look at me. "You are Nathanial Garrett, yes?"

"Nate," I said, shaking her hand. "I'm sorry about what happened to your friends."

"Thank you," Beth said. "Find whoever did it. My mother is a strong woman, I am sure she will recover in time. I'm doing all I can to make sure that her pack...our pack, remain calm. Most of them want to tear the forest apart to hunt for them. I am also sure that someone will try to take advantage of the situation."

"Viktor, by chance?" I asked, taking a shot in the dark.

"He offered his services to find the killer," Logan said. "He has been nothing but supportive of our relationship, why would he wish to disrupt the wedding?"

"Just a thought," Tommy said. "But have you considered it might not be about your wedding?"

"The wolves and lions are together in one place," I said. "Maybe they want to disrupt the truce. Sow dissent among you all. Have you second-guessing everyone. The wedding goes ahead, but people are now full of paranoia and fear. We need to know more, but for now, just go about your day as normal. Well, as much as possible."

"I'm not sure how we can," Beth said. "We were meant to have a banquet tonight, and who wants to go eat when people are being killed? What if the assassin uses it as a way to kill more of us?"

"We'll be there," Tommy said. "Don't worry about that. If the assassin turns up, we'll be prepared."

Logan and Beth both nodded, but I got the impression neither were particularly in the party mood. I couldn't even imagine the stress it was placing on them both, not to mention the fear of further attacks on the people they loved.

I said goodbye and headed out of the courtyard and into the village, stopping outside of the medical hut where Victoria was recovering. There were two huge guards outside, both of whom worked for Tommy, and they nodded as I stepped inside to find a large room with half a dozen beds. Runes adorned the walls, mostly to help with healing and stop any supernatural powers from raging out of control. At the far end of the room, Victoria lay in bed either asleep or unconscious, it was hard to tell.

Sat at her bedside was a woman who appeared to be in her early forties and looked like someone who fought for a living —her bare arms were hard muscle and held more than a few scars. Her chestnut hair was platted with several colored bows.

She looked up at me and got to her feet. She was about my height, and held herself with the air of someone who knew how to break you in half. She reminded me a lot of Diana.

"Mister Garrett?" she asked; her accent was Nordic, but I couldn't have placed it better than that.

"Alexandra," I said. "Or is it Lex? I hear you prefer the latter."

"Lex is fine," she said. "My friend will be okay."

"I hope so. I'm here to talk to her, if we can wake her up."

"The runes keep her asleep, I can break them, but she might not be too pleased when she's awake," Lex said, looking over at Victoria.

"We need answers, she has them," I said. "I'll take the anger directed at me if I need to."

"It will take a few minutes," Lex said as the door burst open, and a much healthier looking Sky walked in.

"We need to talk," Sky said.

"Sky, Lex," I said, introducing the two.

"You're the werelion helping out," Sky said.

"I am," Lex admitted.

"Great," Sky said. "Nate, my brain is less jumbled now."

"You want to go talk?" I asked her.

Sky nodded, and we exited the hut together.

"So, what did you get?" I asked her once we were a short distance away, and I had scanned the area to ensure no one was near.

"The assassin remembered nothing," she told me. "His spirit was a mess, it's why I ended up acting like I was drunk. It was done by a telepath, a powerful one. Whoever it was scrubbed his mind clean of them."

"No telepath I've ever met can remotely blow up someone's head like that," I said.

"No, he was killed some other way," she agreed. "But he'd worked with them for a long time, and this had been planned for a long time too."

"What about the three victims?" I asked.

"That's the thing. Two of them, the males, they knew one another. Varol worked for Vlad the Impaler as a spy, and Kozma worked for the Hungarians, and he was passing along intel to Varol for Vlad."

I sighed; I'd met Vlad once. It had not been fun. "You think they were the target?"

"They met up shortly after arriving here, they needed to get their stories straight about how they'd met," Sky said. "Why would anyone care how two spies met hundreds of years ago?"

"Someone who holds a grudge would care," I said.

CHAPTER SIX

Remy and Diana arrived while Sky and I were talking about what she'd discovered, but before either of them could say anything, Lex stuck her head out of the medical hut and beckoned me over.

"You can't all come in," Lex said.

"We'll wait out here then," Remy said.

"I think the fresh air is probably best for me at the moment," Sky admitted.

Diana said nothing but crossed her arms over her chest while staring at Lex.

"He's safe," Lex said, understanding the not too subtle threat.

"I know," Diana said, her tone hard.

"Your friend doesn't like me," Lex said once I entered the hut.

"She's a werebear," I told her. "I think it's hard to like a species who in the past have actively hunted her kind for sport."

Lex stopped and turned back to me. "We don't do that in my pride." Her voice suggested the topic was off-limits.

"Maybe not," I said, completely ignoring her tone. "But it was pretty widespread during the war between lions and wolves. And Diana is old. Really old."

Lex held my gaze for a heartbeat. "All sides did horrible things during the war."

"That's what people say when they don't want to think about the horrible things their side did."

Lex smiled, although there was no warmth in it. "Yeah, maybe. I've spent centuries trying to make sure we never go back to that point. Some people think they were simpler days."

"Some people are idiots," I said.

"You don't mince your words, do you?"

"I'm not exactly known for keeping my opinions to myself, no," I said. I left off just how much that had gotten me into trouble over the centuries, she didn't need to know.

"Are you going to talk to me, or do I just lie here?" Victoria asked from her bed.

I sat in the chair beside the bed. "I need to know what you can remember."

"You're Nate Garrett, yes?" Victoria asked. "You killed the dragon in London."

"Tiamet," I said. "And I have to keep telling people I didn't do it alone."

"You still killed her," Victoria said. "You stood against Hera. For that, I can trust you."

"You don't like Hera?" I asked.

"I don't like anyone who uses their power to subjugate their own people," Victoria said. "It is stupid and pointless. I'm not a fan of pointless things, Mister Garrett."

"Nate," I said. "And I'd really like it if we could get on

with you telling me what I need to know. People have died."

"The three who were with me," she said. "I remember Kozma being attacked first, I remember him getting two arrows in the back. He turned around then got two more in the chest. I rolled to the side, trying to get to the trees, and then I woke up here. I don't remember anything else. I remember screams though. I'm not sure if they were mine or not."

"Why would someone want those three dead?" I asked. "Did you know them well?"

"I knew Kozma," Victoria said. "We had been together for some time. I knew Varol well enough, and Mona was a sweet woman, kind." Victoria got a faraway look in her eyes before she continued. "I assume you're aware that we were having…fun."

"Was that the first time you were all together?" I asked.

Victoria shook her head. "No. We had been together regularly for the last six months. We all enjoyed each other's company a great deal."

"Would anyone have had a problem with that?" I asked. "Any ex-partners who might take umbrage to your gatherings?"

Victoria laughed. "Gatherings? I haven't heard that one before."

"You'd prefer I said orgy?"

Victoria shook her head. "No, orgy has unpleasant connotations in my mind. Too many people associate it with things that we were not a part of. We were all consenting adults who enjoyed being together. No one was forced, no one was hurt, everyone enjoyed themselves."

"Ever bring in new people?"

"No, not ever," Victoria said firmly.

"I don't care about your sex life," I assured her. "I care that the four of you were together, and that only you survived. I think because you were meant to. I believe one of the other three was the target. Maybe all three of them."

Victoria stared at me for several seconds. She moved into a sitting position, although she remained in bed. "You think I was allowed to survive?"

I nodded. "Yes. The murders were carried out by a professional. There were no tracks, no scents to follow after a period of time, and they used basilisk-tooth-blade-tipped arrows. Yours was apparently coated in manticore venom, which brings a host of new questions. I fought one of the assassins today, he could make clones of himself, and several of them used basilisk-tooth daggers. Whoever is behind this has money and isn't afraid to spend it on the best. If they'd wanted you dead, you'd be dead."

Victoria exhaled sharply and put her head in her hands, her shoulders sagging. "Why leave me alive?" she asked, looking up at me, tears in her eyes.

"I think it's possibly because they needed someone to spread the fear of what had happened. But I think it's more likely you were too important to kill. The mother of the bride, a werewolf with considerable power and clout in the world. They kill you, and maybe Avalon gets involved, maybe your pack tears this realm apart. Your daughter has already told me they're being hard to control."

"She's a strong woman," Victoria said, pride beaming from her. "She will ensure our pack behaves themselves."

"So, you can't remember anything about what happened?" I asked, not wanting the conversation to be steered off topic for too long.

"No," she said. "I heard nothing until Kozma cried out. I saw the arrows sticking out of him. I saw..." Victoria paused and closed her eyes.

"They were in the trees," I said. "Who knew you were

going to the clearing? Anyone? You weren't at the dinner." I turned to Lex, who stood, cross-armed, leaning up against the wall. "Neither of you."

"I decided not to go," Lex said. "I was with Melody."

"Melody is?"

"Viktor's wife," Lex said. "And no, we weren't doing anything. She just hates him, is afraid of him. I don't see her often; her pride is different to my own."

"Where is Viktor now?" I asked.

"Pretending he's important," Lex said. "He's having a conversation with Sven, last I heard."

"Did Viktor have a problem with any of the victims?" I asked.

"I don't know," Victoria said. "I can't tell you."

"You think Viktor did this?" Lex asked.

I shrugged. "I don't know him. I don't know why he'd even want to do this. But I heard he thinks you're sleeping with his wife, so maybe he got the wrong people? He hired them to kill you and Lex, and they screwed up."

"That would be quite the stretch," Lex said.

I nodded. "Probably. There's a lot we don't know." I thought about how Kozma had been hit more than anyone else. How the assassins had cut their throats just to ensure their prey was dead, even though they'd used the basilisk-tooth-bladed arrows to kill them. If Viktor had ordered it, the assassin would surely know what Lex and Melody looked like. No one would be so good as to go to all the effort to stay hidden yet be so incompetent as to murder the wrong people.

"You look lost in thought," Lex said to me.

"I need to go check something. Don't leave the realm."

"Are you commanding that I stay?" Victoria asked with a slight chuckle, and I spotted the smile on Lex's lips.

"I'm pretty sure you're not involved," I said. "But I can tell you this, if I have to find you and you've left this realm, I don't think you'll enjoy me looking for you."

Both women's expressions changed. Neither were happy with the way I'd spoken, but they'd both have to accept it. I wasn't here to make friends; I was here to find a murderer.

"I've been told over the years that you are a fair man," Victoria said as I reached the door.

I turned back to her and nodded. "I'd like to think so."

"I will trust you to do the right thing," she said. "No matter the outcome."

"I don't care about your politics," I said. "I only care about the truth, and getting justice for those whose lives have been taken."

"I hope that's true," Lex said.

"I can't make you believe me," I told her.

"I'm going to stay with Victoria," Lex said. "I know I'm meant to be aiding the investigation, but I assume you don't need my help right now. I think it would be better for independent people to be involved."

"Even though Tommy is a werewolf?" I asked. "And Gordon and Matthew helping?"

"More so," Lex said. "I don't want to believe the lions are involved in this. I will talk to my people and catch up with Gordon and Matthew. I trust them both to be fair. And they trust you."

"I'll let you know what we find," I told her.

I left them to it, and when I walked out of the medical

hut, I found Tommy leaning up against the wall.

"You find out anything useful?" he asked.

"Are you wearing a cowboy hat?"

He flicked the brim of his hat. "My head kept getting snowed on, and this is the only hat they have."

"You're going to start swaggering, aren't you?"

"You going to answer my question?" He asked, putting on a slight Southern American accent.

I shook my head and walked past him, Tommy catching up a moment later. "Nate," he said.

"I don't want to discuss it here," I said. "Let's go back to the murder scene."

"Why?"

"I have a theory I want to check."

As we headed out of the village, we were joined by Sky, Diana, and Remy.

"If I'd have known there would be so much walking involved, I'd have said no when you asked if I wanted to help," Remy said as we walked through the forest toward the clearing.

"It's not the murders you're concerned about?" Diana asked. "It's the walking."

"I have much smaller legs than you," Remy said.

"So, what did you find out?" Sky asked me, ignoring Diana and Remy as they playfully taunted each other.

"Victoria and Lex are innocent," I said. "I can't imagine either of them being involved in what happened here. Sounds like Melody—Viktor's wife—can't stand him."

"Viktor is trying to weasel his way into the investigation," Tommy said. "It sounds like just Lex was asked to be involved, and Viktor sort of inserted himself into it."

"Lex seems more concerned about her friend," I said. "She didn't seem too bothered about actually doing the investigative part. I got the impression she said she'd involve herself just to make sure no one else did."

"I can imagine that's the case," Tommy said. "So, did you find out anything useful?"

As we walked through the forest, I relayed the entire conversation I'd had with Lex and Victoria. Sky went through her own findings again, and by the time we reached the clearing, everyone was caught up.

"So, why are we here?" Remy asked.

"You didn't need to come," I told him. "But as you're here, I want three of you to play victims."

Remy narrowed his eyes. "I am not pretending to be in an orgy."

"No one, and I can't stress this enough, no one is asking you to," I told him.

"You want us to play out where they were when the arrows started flying?" Diana asked.

"I've seen Gordon's preliminary report," Tommy said. "I'm pretty sure we figured out where everyone was when it started."

"And the spirits gave me a pretty good idea of where people were," Sky added. "Also, the longer I'm here, the more the spirits' memories become clearer. Looks like they were still a jumbled mess, and I didn't even realize. Being horrifically murdered really does a number on your spirit, especially when it's several people at once."

The four of them got into their positions, although thankfully even Remy kept his remarks to a minimum.

"So, Tommy is Kozma," I said. "Sky is Victoria, Remy is Varol, and Diana is Mona."

I walked around the four of them as they stood or sat roughly in the spots where the group had been attacked. It wasn't a hundred percent accurate, but then it didn't need to be.

"Right," I said. "Kozma was hit from above twice in the back. Victoria said that he was hit first, she said she remembered the arrows."

"We know the tree where the attack took place," Tommy said, pointing to a large, fifty-foot tree with a thick canopy of leaves.

"We sure?" I asked.

"Yes," Tommy said. "I had my people go up to sniff around. At least one person was sat up there. They used scent blockers, but that still leaves a smell, it just dissipates faster. You remember that sniper in the forest in Germany?"

"The witch?" I asked. "You think magic was used?"

"Runes are carved into the tree," Tommy said. "Not powerful, but they're enough."

"Okay," I said. "Stay where you are." I ran over to the tree, and with my air magic, climbed it without trouble. Finding the branch that had been used by the assassin wasn't hard; the rune carved into the trunk of the tree was dim, the power almost completely gone.

I sat on the branch and looked down at my friends. Tommy was the easiest to see, but beyond that, his bulk blocked the other three from anything close to a good shot. I could make out Remy and Mona, but only their limbs, and Sky was sat in front of Tommy, so she was out too.

"Tommy," I shouted, using air magic to carry my words. "Turn to the left so that Sky can see your back."

Tommy did as I asked, and right there I knew that Victoria hadn't been the intended target. After Tommy moved, Sky had been an open shot.

"Move like Kozma did," I said.

Tommy moved around to the side, a few feet away from where his friends were, and exactly where his body had fallen.

"Sky, you're up," I said.

Sky, as Victoria, rolled to the side, over to Kozma, who had already started to fall, two more arrows in him. Sky reacted like she'd been hit in the shoulder and tried to get to the tree line.

"She wasn't meant to get hit," I said to myself. "Kozma turned too quickly."

I dropped from the tree, air magic slowing my fall, and walked over to everyone.

"How did Mona and Varol move after the initial attack?" I asked.

Sky got to her feet and moved Remy around to face the tree, his arms wide, trying to protect Mona as she moved away.

I watched Diana scramble as Sky had informed her, and lay still when the arrow hit her in the base of her spine.

Sky turned Remy toward Diana, and then instructed him to collapse. Two arrows hit him in the side, one in the ribs, one in the neck. They'd been meant for his torso.

All four victims were no longer a threat, with Kozma probably already dead, and Victoria either running for help, or fleeing out of fear. No matter how tough you are, the need to stay alive can override an awful lot of needs to help your friends.

Mona continued to crawl along the ground until her throat was cut. Varol was on his knees, his throat cut last, after Kozma.

"Varol was forced to watch," I said.

"Varol was the target," Sky said. "I hadn't realized how much of their memories were still jumbled up until I started doing this."

"Forced to watch Mona and Kozma die," Tommy said. "But why? Because he knew Kozma? That seems excessive."

"Victoria was hit by accident," I said.

"Still think she's innocent?" Remy asked, brushing off the snow from his armor.

"The jury has gone back out on that one," I said. "Sky's right though, Varol was the target. He was killed last; he was kneeling as Mona was murdered."

"His memory is clearer," Sky said. "No faces of the killers, they wore balaclavas, or masks. Something like that. He watched Mona die. He watched Kozma die. He was forced to linger on both of them, shouted at."

"We just don't know why," Diana said.

"Or who did it," Remy said. "Or who hired them. Or how that guy's head exploded like a water balloon."

"You ever considered motivational speaking?" Tommy asked him.

"I'm only saying we don't know a lot," Remy said.

"Victoria is our next stop," Sky said. "Something is off here."

I walked to where Mona's body had been found. "Tommy, there's a guardian who lets people out of this realm, yes?" I looked over at him for an answer.

"You know there is," Tommy said. "I have two people going to talk to both of them. One man, one woman, they work in shifts. I'm on it, trust me."

"You're thinking they let the killer in?" Diana asked.

I nodded. "Either they have another of those bloody irritating tablet things that took us to Nidavellir, or they came through the main realm gate. Or there's another gate, and they've figured out a way to use it."

Guardians were linked to a realm gate, and until we'd discovered the lost Norse dwarves, they'd been the only people capable of operating a realm gate. They were essentially immortal when around the gate, but the farther they moved from it, the less powerful they became. If there was a second realm gate, and it had been activated, they'd hopefully know.

"I'm going to return to the village and get Sorcery," I said. "And then I'm going to check out this forest."

"Alone?" Diana asked. "Yeah, I don't see that happening. I'll join you."

"We can't say for a hundred percent certain that Victoria was accidentally hit," Sky said. "I'm going off the memories of three dead people, and it wasn't a fun experience. I've probably said it before, but murdered spirits are notoriously unreliable."

"I know, but we don't have a lot to go on," I said. "We need information."

We were walking back to the village when Matthew appeared in the trail ahead. "You've been hard to find," he said. "We have a problem."

"Oh good, another one," Remy said.

"What's happened?" Tommy asked.

"It's Viktor," Matthew said. "He's been murdered."

"Fan-fucking-tastic," Remy muttered to himself.

CHAPTER SEVEN

To say that Viktor had been murdered was doing the word murdered an injustice. He'd been nailed to the side of the barn with two-foot-long silver daggers through his wrists, his feet had been cut off, and another dagger had been rammed up under his chin into his brain. There was a large pool of blood under him, and from the looks of the arterial spray on the wall where he'd been nailed, Viktor had been alive when his feet were removed.

"That's a lot of effort to kill one person," Tommy whispered as we stood in front of Viktor's corpse while Gordon instructed half a dozen realm staff to safely lower the body to the ground.

"They crucified him, cut off his feet, and then stabbed him under the chin," I said. "What's the point? And why cut his feet off? Why crucify him? The effort alone would be huge."

I looked around the area, which was beginning to get a larger and larger crowd that were being held back closer to the castle by a combination of Tommy's people and the realm staff. It was getting late and most of the stable-hands had been cleaning out the stalls or seeing to the animals. Viktor had been killed in a spot some distance from the main stable.

"How did no one hear him scream?" I asked.

"Hello," Tommy shouted, getting everyone in the nearby area to turn around and look at him. He waved and turned back to the grizzly scene. "I think people would hear screaming. No one is so mentally strong that they can withstand being crucified, having their feet removed, and from the looks of him, having the shit kicked out of them first."

"Who found the body?" I asked.

"Stable-hand," Gordon said. "Poor kid is only nineteen. No one should ever see shit like this, but at nineteen, it's unthinkable."

I spotted the stable-hand in question, Sky crouched before him at the far end of the stables. She'd given him a large mug, probably coffee with lots of sugar. The kid looked like he might vomit at any moment, but to his credit he was answering questions.

"How did no one hear?" I asked.

"He was drugged," Gordon said. "I can smell it. Same stuff in Victoria."

"Manticore venom," Tommy said.

"An insurance policy," I said with a sigh. "We're pretty sure that Varol was the target in the forest."

"Don't know him," Gordon said, washing his bloody hands in a nearby bucket of water, which quickly turned red. "He worked for Vlad the Impaler a few centuries ago. And that was one person the world could have done without. I'm all for laying waste to your enemies, but I'm not sure that murdering your own people just to show your enemies how crazy you are, is a long-term strategy."

"It worked," Tommy said.

"For a while," Gordon said. "And now he'll forever be known as a monster. Or hero. It really depends on who you ask."

"Okay, moving on," I said. "We need this entire place in lockdown. No one comes, no one goes."

"Already given the order," Tommy said. "That was before this was done though, so I'll see how it's going. The realm has its own guard, but by their own admission, they're completely out of their depth."

I watched Viktor's body—now draped in a black cloth—wheeled away on a gurney. The large pool of blood under where he'd been found would remain until it could be cleaned. It was starting to freeze, the cold already making a hard job even more difficult.

"Where's his wife?" I asked.

Matthew and Sky had joined us, and all four of them turned to me.

"Melody," I said. "Where's Melody?"

"You think Melody did this?" Gordon asked.

"I think the first person you look at in a murder when you have no suspects, is their spouse."

"She's up in her room," Matthew said. "Or should be. They were all told to stay inside."

"She's my destination then," I said.

"I've already sent some of my people to see her," Tommy told me. "I haven't heard back, but there should be guards outside. Room 419."

"You still seeing the guardian?" I asked him.

Tommy nodded. "I've got people searching the victims' rooms, including Victoria's. Hopefully, we turn something up."

"I'll go with him," Matthew said.

"Oh, before I forget," Gordon said. "Sorry, it's been a bit hectic. I know what killed that assassin. There were trace amounts of explosives in his remains. He'd been wearing an earbud for communications."

"An explosive earbud?" I asked.

"There wouldn't need to be a lot," Sky said. "And if you put runes on the earbud, you could increase the power of the explosion."

"Any chance you found runes?" Tommy asked.

"I found pieces of transparent plastic," Gordon said. "Any runes would have been destroyed though."

"At least we know they're using a comms system to communicate," I said. "Although, that in and of itself is weird. Technology doesn't travel through realms well."

"A rune-based comms system?" Sky suggested. "I've used one before, but not in something that small."

"And just to compound the misery," Gordon said. "I tested the other victims for the same agent in Victoria and Viktor. None of the three had any paralyzing agent in their bodies. There would still be traces considering they died so quickly after being stabbed. You'd expect to find something. The manticore venom was only used on those two."

I filed the information away for later use. "Let's go see Melody," I said.

Sky accompanied me into the castle, and through the empty hallways as we took the stairs to the fourth floor, where we found half a dozen of Tommy's people. Two were walking down the hallway, while another two stood either side of the stairs at the far end, and two more were stationed outside a room about halfway down the hall.

I turned to the large windows beside me, looked over the courtyard below. The forest spread out in the distance, and I was pretty sure I could make out where the first three murders had taken place.

"You okay?" Sky asked, touching my arm to bring my attention back to her.

I nodded. "Something feels all wrong about this."

"About what? The murders?"

"Viktor's murder," I said. "The three killings earlier were professional, quick, clean. Varol might have been the victim, but the deaths were done without fanfare, without the need to grandstand. Viktor was tortured, the position of his body was designed to be a public humiliation."

"Maybe the killers were hired to do two different types of murder," Sky said.

"That's possible," I told her. "I've seen professional killers do such things before, but he was beaten, drugged, crucified, his feet cut off, then murdered. That's a different set of skills to being an assassin."

"I need to tell you something," she said. "I tried to reach out to Viktor's spirit. I got nothing but a swirl of darkness. Whatever they did to him, his spirit is a mess."

I sighed. "I did wonder. I wasn't going to ask you to look into another spirit after the mess of the last few."

"I did it on the sly," Sky said with a smile. "I'd rather not try again until we know what was actually done to his spirit."

"We're not exactly inundated with clues, are we?"

"Let's go ask Melody," Sky said, setting off down the hallway.

I jogged to catch up, and we stopped outside room 419, where the two guards—one male and one female—nodded to us and pushed open the door, letting us inside.

"Nice," Sky said as we stepped into what was a suite. A large living area directly in front, with a door on the left that sat ajar and showed a bathroom beyond; a closed door on the right that I assumed was the bedroom.

The room was furnished with a comfortable looking leather sofa, several dark wooden units, and a small library next to a drinks' cabinet. There were two glass doors directly opposite the entrance, and a balcony beyond.

"Melody," Sky shouted. "We need to talk."

The door to the bedroom opened and a young woman —or at least someone who looked like a young woman—stepped out. She had long blonde hair that flowed over her shoulders, and wore a black t-shirt, and dark blue jeans. Her feet were bare, and she padded over to the nearby bar, grabbed a tumbler, a bottle of rum, and poured herself a generous portion.

"To Viktor," she said, her accent putting her from Germany, or maybe Austria. She knocked back the drink, poured another. "The fucking cunt."

"This is going to go brilliantly," Sky whispered.

"Melody," I said. "I assume you know about your husband."

"Yes, good," Melody said. "I hope it fucking well hurt."

"Not a fan?" Sky asked.

"Viktor was controlling, mean, unpleasant, a bully, a thug, violent, and a whole lot more. I was a prisoner in my own goddamned home, brought out to look pretty and show the world his prize." Melody poured a third drink. "Whatever they did to him, he deserved it."

"Do you know what they did to him?" I asked.

Melody shook her head. "He's dead, that's all I care about."

Sky told her exactly what had been done to Viktor and Melody laughed. "They cut off his feet?" Was all she could say.

"Is that symbolic in some way?" I asked.

"He had it done to a few werewolves who crossed him," Melody said. "Take a foot, use silver to do it. Foot might grow back in a few decades, but the memory of what had been done would last a lifetime."

"Anyone here today have that done?" I asked.

"I don't know," Melody said, downing her fourth shot. "Probably. He pissed off everyone he ever met. You spoken to Lex? She hated him too."

"Yeah, I get that," I said. "Victoria hate him too?"

Melody stared at me for a moment. "Everyone hated him."

"What about the three murders in the forest?" I asked. "Did everyone hate Varol and Mona too? What about Kozma?"

"Kozma was nice," Melody said. "I didn't know Mona, although I heard she was sweet. Varol was... Varol was very good, if you know what I mean. I'm sadder about his death than Viktor's."

"You and he had a relationship?" Sky asked.

"We did," she said. "A long time ago, before I met Viktor."

"I assume Viktor wasn't happy about it," I said.

"No, he was not," Melody said. "In fact, he hated it. He had to do business with Varol's pride, and to say that he was unhappy about it was an understatement. The idea of another man taking what was his, even if it was well before we'd even met, was a betrayal."

"I'm sorry for what you went through," Sky said.

"Viktor was a pig," Melody said. "But now I'm free, and I won't be staying around that pride of his. Lex has offered to take me into hers, and I will accept that offer." Melody smiled for the first time.

"Where is Viktor's pride right now," I asked. "I haven't seen any of the members."

"They weren't allowed entry," Melody said. "Too many of them would immediately start a fight or they would do something stupid. His pride is full of those who have been kicked out of other prides for their behavior. They're criminals, thugs, and bullies. Just like him."

I looked out of the nearby window at the mountains in the distance, the forest that surrounded it. I wondered if the assassins were out there right now, waiting for further prey.

"Could Viktor have had the three of them murdered?" I asked, turning back to Melody.

"He'd have wanted to be involved," she said. "He'd have wanted to see Varol for himself. See the pain in his eyes."

"What if someone let him see it?" I asked. "A telepath?"

Melody thought for a second. "He might have, yes," she said. "But he was too busy fighting with the other guests to really pay attention to it."

"The whole time?" I asked.

"No, after his brother burst in, he sat there quiet as a mouse."

"The brother the one with the big beard?" I asked.

"That's him," Melody said. "Father of the groom. His name is Sven Rohmer. He's German, like me and Viktor."

"And what's he like?" I asked.

"Sven is a good man," Melody said. "Doesn't have a pride, but everyone knows not to pick a fight with him. He loves Logan and Beth a great deal. I think he only invited Viktor because he wanted to help me get some time away from his sycophants."

"You and Sven ever had a relationship?" Sky asked.

Melody laughed. "No, not ever. He hated Viktor though. They were brothers, but Viktor was always jealous, always angry. If Viktor had those people killed, I'm surprised he didn't have Sven and Lex killed too."

"Has anyone seen Sven?" I asked.

"I'll go check," Sky told me, and left the room in a hurry.

"You're Nate Garrett, aren't you?" Melody asked when we were alone. "Tommy's friend."

I nodded.

"What would you do to me if I had killed my abusive husband?"

I stared at her for several seconds. "I don't know. I think we'd have to figure out how much of your story was true then go from there. I'm not saying I don't believe you, but there's a difference between believing you, and letting you go for your husband's murder."

"And if he'd attacked me and I'd killed him in self-defense?"

I shrugged. "He was nailed to a wall. That's going beyond self-defense."

"How many people have you killed, Nate?"

"A lot," I told her. "And if I'd murdered someone and nailed them to a wall, I'd expect a few people to want to know why. Look, Viktor was an arsehole, I get it, I don't much care that he's dead. I don't much care that he was tortured, but I do care about three people murdered in a forest for no goddamned reason. If Viktor did it, I guess this whole thing is all wrapped up, but I need to find out why. Because, and please don't take offence, I don't think it was about you."

"I'm not entirely sure how to take that," Melody said.

"You're his wife," I told her. "He is, in your own words, a thug and bully. And also, I assume, you were still sleeping with Varol, yes?"

"His pride and Varol's did business," Melody said. "There may have been a few occasions."

"If Viktor knew, he'd want you to watch as your lover died."

Melody considered it. "Yes, that's true, he would."

"So, if he was involved, it wasn't about you," I said, looking out of the window again at the balcony. "At least, it wouldn't be totally about you. That's saying it was Viktor at all. And it's not like we can ask him."

"Your friend is a necromancer," she said.

"Viktor's spirit is all messed up," I said, and looked over to the balcony again as snow flurries began, first in small clumps, and then as a larger drift.

I took a step toward the window as the door to the suite opened and a tall and broad white man with a long, thick dark beard, and hair of the same color tied back from his face, stepped into the room. He wore a dark blue suit, the jacket open to reveal the white shirt beneath. He placed his hands in his pockets when he saw me.

"Sven," Melody said as the big man walked over and hugged her.

I turned back to the balcony, but the snowfall was done. There had probably been a buildup on the roof, I'd seen it happen in my own room a few times.

"Are you done questioning Melody?" Sven said, regaining my attention.

"You and your brother didn't get along," I said, making sure Sven understood it wasn't a question.

"He was an unpleasant man," Sven said, clearly choosing his words carefully.

"You didn't answer my question," I replied.

"No, Mister Garrett," Sven said, tersely. "We didn't get along."

"Why invite him then?" I asked.

"Because he was still my brother, still my son's uncle," Sven said with a slight sigh. "We managed to ban his pride, but to not invite Viktor would have been a large slight on my part. Beth and Logan didn't need that when starting their new life together."

I nodded as if thinking long and hard about the answer. "And the three killed in the forest?"

"I've already spoken to Tommy's people about this," Sven said.

"And now you're talking to me," I told him, keeping my voice light. There was no need to escalate tensions, especially with those tensions being high as they were.

"I didn't know any of them well," Sven said. "I'd met Mona a few times, and knew Varol by reputation, but that was it. Never met Kozma until he showed up with Victoria. She is a little high maintenance, but she's nice enough."

"What about her ex-husband?" I asked. "The one arguing with Viktor."

"I don't know him at all," Sven said. "He was a blowhard as much as Viktor. I haven't spent a second of time in his company. His name is Luke Kratz, you're more than welcome to go find him and talk to him yourself, good luck getting him to say anything that isn't swearing."

"I'm good," I said and walked toward the door before stopping and turning back to Sven and Melody. "Just one more thing." I felt like I should be wearing a trench coat for full effect.

Both looked over at me.

"There have been four murders now," I said. "And Gordon told me that Victoria had the same paralyzing agent in her body that Viktor had. Manticore Venom."

"So, it's the same killers," Sven said confidently. "Go find them."

"Yeah, here's the thing," I said. "None of the other three victims had the paralyzing agent, so why do you think the killers would use a bit on Viktor and Victoria, but not on the others?"

"I don't know," Sven said, his brow dropping into a frown as if pondering the question.

"Me neither," I told him. "But I'm going to find out, and I'll let you know what I discover."

"Please do, Mister Garrett," Sven said, just as the doors to the balcony exploded inward, raining shards of glass as I dove behind a large chair.

CHAPTER EIGHT

My ears rang. I wasn't entirely sure if it was from the explosion or if there was another reason I hadn't discovered, but the ringing made my head hurt, and screwed with my balance enough that I sat behind the large black armchair and blinked as I watched Sven and Melody sprint into the bedroom.

It didn't take long for my ears to stop ringing, and I got to my feet to find two black-clad individuals, both wearing masks similar to that worn by the assassin in the morgue. One of the assassin's was male, the other female. The male was at least a foot and a half taller than the woman, and much broader. The woman had the mouth portion of the mask completely removed, revealing bright purple lipstick.

"You here to kill me or them?" I asked, pointing toward the bedroom door.

The woman screamed at me, and I was thrown back into the wall behind me, my ears ringing again. Banshee.

I rolled aside, hoping that I could get to the banshee before she shattered my eardrums and made me vomit up my own organs. I do not like fighting banshees, they are not pleasant.

The scream cut through the chair I'd crouched behind, and I wrapped myself in a shield of air, before jumping out, just as she screamed again, the force of the concussive sound almost pushing me back. I threw my shield forward, turning it into a battering ram, which forced the banshee to throw herself aside rather than be smashed to the ground.

Her partner was tearing apart the door in an effort to get to the two werelions inside, which at least meant he was a problem for future Nate, and I could concentrate on my more immediate issue.

The banshee screamed again, but I was already moving around to the side of her. She followed me, her mouth open, the scream tearing into the floor and furniture as if it was a tornado of sound. She turned on the spot, never letting me out of her sight as I moved closer to the windows, the crunch of glass under my feet barely audible. The banshee took a deep breath, stopping the scream just long enough for me to throw a dagger of fire at her throat.

A banshee's neck is reinforced muscle, which makes it almost impossible to kill them by cutting their throat, but I wasn't trying to kill her, just shut her up.

The dagger lodged in her neck, thankfully stopping the sonic power. I snapped my fingers, and the dagger exploded, the tip of which was still in her neck. Blood poured down her front from the newly created hole.

She acted like the wound barely bothered her, and darted toward me, a dagger in each hand. I had time to notice that they were basilisk-tooth blades, and moved through the ruined glass to the balcony as the door to the suite burst open and Sky ran inside.

"I'm good," I called out, and Sky raced toward the male assassin, who had finished tearing the door apart and was now inside the bedroom, the noises of fighting easy to hear.

Once outside in the fresh air, and with the female assassin still trying to stick a blade in somewhere I'd rather she didn't,

I walked backwards, along the balcony, dodging her swipes and lunges.

"Why aren't you fighting?" she asked. Her neck had already healed, and she took a step back, rolling her shoulders.

"Tired?" I asked her. "Looks like you've lost a lot of blood."

"Not enough to stop me killing you," she said with a snarl.

Thunder rumbled above. "Just so you know, this isn't going to make me feel very happy."

"You'll be dead," she said with a smirk. "You'll get over it."

I shrugged as I raised one hand to the clouds. Lightning streaked down from the skies, and slammed into my outstretched hand, turning it into a charred mess in an instant. The lightning travelled through my body, mixing with my magic, and left through the hand that was pointing directly at the banshee.

She noticed the danger she was in an instant before the lightning left my fingertips and smashed into her like a freight train. It hit her in the upper chest and throat, removed a large part of her torso, leaving nothing but the smell of burned flesh and hair.

The banshee dropped to the ground in a heap. I wasn't entirely sure whether or not she was dead, but the blade of fire I conjured to remove her head made sure of it. I looked back inside the suite as Sky rammed a silver dagger into the temple to the male assassin, while Sven leaned against the nearby wall, his werelion form matted with blood.

"Everyone okay?" I asked as I stepped back inside. My hand would take a little while to heal, but thankfully my magic made sure the pain was the first thing to go.

"Fine," Sven said, getting back to his full height. "Blood

is mostly his."

"What is he?" I asked, prodding the assassin's body with the tip of my boot.

"Sorcerer," Sky said, sounding a little out of breath. "Could use matter magic. Made him strong and fast, but thankfully, not strong or fast enough."

"Are they after me?" Melody asked from the bedroom door.

"Let's go find out," I said. I left the suite and stood over the dead banshee, letting out a big sigh.

"You don't have to do this," Sky said, standing where the windows had once been. "I can..."

"You've done enough," I told her. "I'll take this one."

"What are you talking about?" A now human-looking Sven asked as he comforted Melody.

"I'm part necromancer," I said. "I can absorb spirits, but I take all their memories too. It only works on those who have been killed in battle, but I think this counts."

"I'll wait for you," Sky said, taking a seat on the nearby sofa, which had miraculously remained largely unscathed during the fighting.

I reached out with my necromancy, feeling for the spirit of the dead assassin. My fingers went cold, and there was a shiver up my arm, leaving pins and needles in its place as the spirit was grabbed by my power and dragged into me. Her memories flooded me, rich and dark and vile, dropping me to my knees. The spirit would make my own magic more powerful, but the downside was having to relive every single shitty thing the recently-deceased had ever done. Every good thing too, but it's rare that someone dies fighting at my hands because they were just too goddamned good.

The banshee didn't have a name, not one that I could pronounce anyway, it was a banshee name, a sound created with their power. She'd killed hundreds: men, women, even children. She'd killed for fun, then killed for whoever paid her the most money. She had no loyalty to anyone or anything, she didn't much care about anyone or anything, although she considered the group of assassins she'd been working with for the last few decades to be as close to family as she was ever likely to have. The assassin who made clones was Leon. The head assassin was a man by the name of Farkas Tibor, a Hungarian national who had brought all these assassins together to make money and kill people.

Farkas and his team of five arrived in the realm several days ago, they'd walked through the realm gate easy as you please, and the banshee noticed Farkas handing something to someone inside the realm gate temple as the team went to the forest to prepare.

There was a lot of erroneous stuff about how much money they were being paid, but the banshee kept mostly to herself. She saw Farkas talking to Viktor more than once in the forest but had no interest in the matter one way or the other. The morning of the murders, Farkas knew Victoria would be having a rendezvous in the forest, knew that Kozma and Varol would be there too. There was no mention of Mona, but Farkas told them Victoria was not to die. He had made that very clear.

I came to, and found myself sitting on the ground, next to the body of the banshee.

"Ten minutes," Sky said. "You okay?"

I nodded. "Victoria was to be kept alive," I said, getting to my feet.

"She was in on it?" Sky asked.

"No," I said, noticing the expression of concern on Sven's face. "Anything you want to add, Sven?" I asked.

"Victoria would not have led Kozma to his death," Sven told me.

"She didn't," I said. "Looks like the head of the assassins is someone called Farkas Tibor, he's a sorcerer with some mind magic. He dressed up as a waiter and walked around the hotel, getting close enough to put the suggestion in the heads of Kozma, Mona, Victoria, and Varol. The four had been intimate before, so it didn't take much. The assassins lie in wait, the happy foursome come to have some fun, and they get killed. The banshee was ordered to let Victoria live, in her boss's words, 'we're not here for her, and we don't need that level of trouble'."

"They must have been worried when they hit her with an arrow," Sky said.

"The dead guy on the floor here did that," I said. "The clone guy came back to the village to make sure Victoria didn't die on the way. It shook them all up."

"Anything else?" Sky asked.

"Varol was definitely the intended target," I said.

"Any idea why?" Sky asked, leaning forward in her seat.

"I think it has something to do with Vlad the Impaler, although the banshee didn't know enough to make me sure."

"Vlad is dead," Sven said.

"But grudges go on a long time," I replied.

"Did you see who hired them?" Sky asked.

I shook my head. "No, but they're here. The banshee saw her boss talking to someone but couldn't make out who it was."

"His name is Peter," Melody blurted out. "No, I will not be quiet," she snapped at Sven who tried to shush her.

"Sven," I said softly. "Let her talk."

"The assassin there," Melody said. "His name is Peter. I

don't know his last name. He worked for Viktor."

"Were these Viktor's personal assassins?" Sky asked.

"No idea," Melody said. "Only ever seen Peter here."

"And why is this information you want to stop her sharing?" Sky asked Sven.

"Because there's an assassin still out there, and they tried to kill her," Sven said. "She needs to be as far from this as possible."

"They were sent to kill her," I confirmed. "And you, Sven."

"Me?" Sven asked, bemused by the idea. "Why kill me?"

"Because you're Viktor's brother," I said. "The banshee had seen a list. Melody and you were both on it. This hit must have cost them a lot of money."

"Any more names on that list?" Sky asked.

"No," I said with a shake of my head. "Just you two and Varol. She didn't ask why, although I assume it's because, at least in part, Melody was cheating on Viktor with Varol, and Sven knew about it. I'm right, aren't I?"

Sven nodded.

"You helped facilitate it," Sky said. "You were their go-between."

"Not just with Varol," I said as little flickers of the banshee's memories continued to work their way to the front of my mind. "Lex."

Melody's expression told me all I needed to know.

"You were arranging with Lex to run away," I said. "Viktor found out."

"So, why not kill Lex?" Sky asked.

"Same reason he can't kill Victoria," I said. "Melody is his pride, Sven has no pride, and Varol was something else, but Lex and Victoria both belong to a strong pride and pack respectively, if one of them is murdered, there would be outrage. There'd be a group of exceptionally powerful and angry weres looking for justice or vengeance. Can't risk killing them. It's why the banshee was so freaked out when Victoria took an arrow to the back."

"Are you sure it was Viktor who hired them?" Sven asked.

I nodded. "The banshee saw Farkas talking to Viktor a few times. She didn't know if Viktor was hiring him, but it definitely looked like it. There's someone at the realm gate temple who's in on it too. I'll go find Tommy and let him know, we can take the person into custody and figure out exactly what happened here."

"Anything about Viktor being a target?" Sky asked.

"No," I said. "He wasn't on the list; he wasn't killed when the banshee was there. She was too busy scaling the damn castle. If Viktor was one of their targets, he was a secret one. Sky, can you get every one of the main guests here into the dining hall. I think it would be safer. That includes you two."

"Of course," Melody said. "We'll head right there."

"Yes," Sven said.

Sky looked over at Melody and Sven and back to me. "I'll make sure they get there and go check on Tommy's people. We should be able to gather up the majority of wedding guests."

"Good, that way we can make sure they're all safe," I lied, and was pretty sure that Sky knew I was lying, but she went along with it, which was a testament to how long we'd known each other, and the trust we held.

"I don't need anyone looking after me," Sven said.

"It's not open for discussion," I told him. "I want to know where everyone is at all times. There's still at least one assassin in the realm, and there's nothing to say that Viktor was a target, which means possibly a second killer. You're going to go to the hall or I'm going to drag you there, and I don't think you'd like that."

"Do not threaten me," Sven said, his voice like iron.

"Not a threat," I said. "That's just what's going to happen. I'd rather it not, but if you're going to put the lives of others in jeopardy, I'm going to deal with you accordingly. Werelion or not, I doubt you want to get into a fight with a sorcerer who has had an exceptionally long day."

"He'll go," Melody said, clearly the voice of reason. "No one needs anymore problems or fighting here. We just need to catch those responsible so Beth and Logan can have a nice wedding."

"We will continue this conversation at another opportunity," Sven said.

I shrugged. I didn't much care what he did, and walked over to the door, opening it as Sky joined me. "You think they can still hear me?" she asked as we both stepped into the hallway.

I nodded, but there was little to do about it. "I think this isn't done by a long shot." I looked out one of the windows. "I think the assassin's leader is out there. And I think there's more to this than just Viktor wanting a bit of revenge."

"So, you've settled on Viktor hiring them?" Sky asked.

"The banshee saw him talking to the assassin's leader more than once, so yeah, I think Viktor hired them. But I don't think Viktor was killed by them. I'm going to go talk to Victoria again as I have questions, and then I'm going to find Tommy and figure out what happened with the guardian he went to talk to."

"And after that?" Sky asked, leaning up against the window I had stared out earlier.

"I think after that, I'm going to hopefully know where this assassin is, and we can put this whole nightmare to bed."

"Do you know who killed Viktor?"

I shrugged. "Got an idea, but no evidence so I'll keep it to myself for the moment."

"I have an idea too," Sky told me.

"You're not going to tell me, are you?" I asked her.

"Nope," Sky said with a smile. "Because I don't want anyone to hear me, and I don't want to be wrong."

I laughed. "Because I'd never let you forget it?"

"Yes, Nate, exactly because of that," Sky said with a laugh of her own. "This whole thing is a mess, but you know the one thing that bothers me? Viktor didn't bring a single member of his pride here. I know that he wasn't allowed to bring anyone, but Viktor didn't strike me as someone who did as they were told. Why would you not bring anyone from your pride? He's their leader, and he's taking his wife with him. I'm sure he felt safe, but would Matthew have come here without some of his people if Tommy hadn't been here?"

"No," I said.

"And Viktor must know that he wasn't the most liked person, he certainly should have known Melody hated him," Sky said. "Either that or he didn't care. I just find it odd that he knew he was going somewhere he was at best distrusted, and still agreed to come without backup."

"It's his own family," I said. "Maybe he thought that was enough."

"He was wrong then," Sky said.

I nodded. "Be careful."

"I'm a big girl, Nate," Sky told me.

"Yeah, but even so, be careful."

"You too," Sky said, suddenly serious.

I left the castle via the front door and walked through to the stables where the remnants of Viktor's blood was being washed away by staff members. They'd had a shitty day, and it probably wasn't near done yet.

Sorcery was outside the stable with a hand getting her saddled, so I stopped by and fed her a huge apple from the bucket. "Any chance you could tell me what's going on?" I asked her.

"Sorry, sir, I don't know," the young stable-hand said.

"Sorry," I replied. "Talking to the horse, but thanks for letting me know."

Sorcery nuzzled my neck and I scratched her behind the ear, while giving her a second apple. She was still saddled, and looked like she was about to go for a ride.

"She just coming back, or just going?" I asked.

"She's just about to go," the stable-hand said. "I have to take her out once a day for a good run through the forest. They get really irritated if they don't get their daily exercise.

"I didn't mean to keep you from your job," I said.

I watched the stable-hand lead Sorcery toward the gates to the village as a commotion further in the village caught my attention.

A figure was running toward the bridge where Sorcery was being led. The man moved fast—faster than few people I'd ever seen—almost a blur of motion. They passed me and a second later a large wolf ran toward me too, chasing the fleeing figure.

"Tommy?" I asked.

He snorted and continued on, barely stopping for a moment.

I ran after him, considerably slower than a werewolf was able to run, and used my air magic to jump up, placing my hands on Sorcery's flank and vaulting into her saddle.

"Sorry, but I need to borrow her," I told the stable-hand, who passed me the reins.

"Let's go do some cowboy shit," I said to Sorcery, and we chased after Tommy and his prey.

CHAPTER NINE

Even with Sorcery's incredible speed, we were still some distance behind Tommy and whoever he was chasing. I'd wrapped myself in a shield of air, which deflected any branches that got a little too close for comfort. It seemed that however fast Sorcery had run the first time we'd made the journey, apparently she'd been really holding back.

The sounds of the wind whipping by me blocked out the battle into which Sorcery charged. I created a lasso of air, flicked it out toward the man as he dove toward Tommy, a silver dagger in each hand.

The lasso caught around the man's ankle and I yanked back, throwing him across the clearing. He threw a knife at me and I launched myself off Sorcery and blasted the man with a bolt of lightning that sent him sprawling across the clearing where three murders had taken place only a short time ago. Tommy had been wise enough to launch himself into the tree line as the lightning had hit, avoiding any splash damage.

"Tommy," I called out, and a large dark wolf padded out of the forest beside me.

"Took you long enough," he said with a chuckle.

"You're one of the guardians," I said to the man as he got

to his feet. "Didn't know you could move that fast."

"We all have our gifts," he said.

"You want to tell us why you're working with assassins?" I asked him.

"They paid me," he said without any remorse.

"Four people are dead," Tommy snapped.

"Three of whom deserved nothing less," the guardian snapped back.

"Which one didn't?" I asked as I moved to the side, putting distance between myself and Tommy. Standing together would have presented one large target, and I wanted the guardian to be nervous.

"Mona," the guardian said. "I didn't know they were going to kill her."

"And the others?" Tommy asked.

"Those people died because of Vlad," the guardian said.

"Vlad is dead," I said.

"And those of us who aren't human have long memories of what he did to my people," the guardian said, his eyes darting between Tommy and me, his knuckles white from his grip on his one remaining dagger.

"You knew that Kozma and Varol were going to be here," I said. "So, you hired the assassins?"

"You won't understand," the guardian shouted, his emotions bubbling over, as I spotted the glyphs drawn onto the backs of his hands.

"You're a witch," I said. "You're using a lot of power, that's a big chunk of your life gone."

"I'm a guardian," he said with an air of smugness. "Turns out, I'm immortal so long as I stay close to the realm gate, but I can still use my witch magic."

"Lucky you," Tommy said after he'd taken a step closer to the guardian.

"Why don't you explain to me why you wanted Kozma and Varol dead?" I asked. "You said that Vlad hurt your people. Kozma and Varol were spies, they were trading secrets about Ottoman forces."

"I'm from Targoviste," the guardian said, the words coming with obvious difficulty. "Twenty thousand of my people were... impaled outside of the city. My family among them. Kozma and Varol worked together to ensure Vlad's sadism was put on full display." The guardian's tone was full of hurt and anger, and I wondered how long he'd kept everything bottled up.

"They traded lives for coin! Coin!" he continued, his voice rising with every word. "Kozma might have sold the secrets to Varol, but Varol knew what Vlad would do to those people he captured. Innocent people."

The guardian started to weep, and I took a step forward and he fell to his knees.

"You hired Viktor?" Tommy asked.

"No," the guardian said, wiping his nose with his arm. "No, Viktor is...was aligning himself with a pack in Hungary. Many of those there are descendants of Vlad's tyranny. Viktor and the other pride leader were here for a meeting about a year ago, I overheard them talking. When I saw the guest list for the wedding, and both Kozma and Varol were on it, I knew I had to do something. I contacted Viktor, and he took the opportunity to use his connections to gain closer ties with the other pack."

"They offered Viktor money, didn't they?" I asked.

"Viktor was being paid a million dollars for this assassination," the guardian said. "He offered me a cut. I didn't take it. This wasn't about the money. It was about justice."

"Justice for your family," Tommy said. "I get that. I'd want justice too, but they killed Mona. She was innocent."

"I told Viktor no innocent people," the guardian said.

"What's your name?" I asked.

"Cem," he said softly. The dagger the guardian held finally dropped to the ground. "I didn't want anyone innocent to die, I just wanted justice. I just wanted them to pay for what they'd helped cause."

I collected Cem's daggers as Tommy towered over the guardian.

"Is that why you had them kill Viktor?" I asked. "He went back on his word about killing innocent people."

Cem looked up at me, his face awash with tears. "No, I never even saw the assassins. Never had any contact with them. You need to know something though. They weren't alone."

"The assassins?" Tommy asked. "What do you mean they weren't alone?"

"Viktor's pride is here," Cem said. "They've been arriving steadily for weeks. There are a dozen of them. They only came through when I was in charge of the realm gate, and there were no documents to declare them. They've been living in the forest."

"Why?" I asked, with a sudden itch on the back of my neck that made me glance around the clearing.

"Viktor said he needed them," Cem said. "He said they were his backup if anything went south. If the plan didn't work and Kozma and Varol escaped justice and fled into the forest, the lions could track them."

"A dozen werelions?" Tommy asked, also looking around the edge of the clearing. "There's no way he'd hire expensive assassins, and then bring his people here. Why not just get them to do the job?"

"He had another plan for them," I said. "We need to get back to the village, I think this whole thing was going to be Viktor's way to eliminate everyone he hates in one go."

"Red Wedding style?" Tommy asked.

"I don't know what that means, but probably," I told him.

Tommy sighed. "Get your enemies somewhere together under a banner of peace to enjoy themselves, and have them all murdered."

"That sounds about right, yes," I said.

The sound of clapping came from behind, and I turned to find a man clad in black leather armor and black mask, strolling toward us.

"Well, aren't you just the clever little detectives," the black-clad man said, removing their mask.

Farkas, the leader of the assassins.

"You murdered at least three people," Tommy said. "Possibly four, we haven't discounted Viktor's own murder."

"We don't kill the man who pays us," Farkas said. "We had four targets, the two men here, his brother, and wife."

"Your guys are dead," I told him. "Did it myself. The clone guy too. You need much better people."

"I don't know who you are, but you'll wish you hadn't involved yourself," Farkas said, drawing two basilisk-tooth blades from sheaths on his hip.

"You're going to tell us what we need to know," Tommy said, cracking his neck as he moved his head from side to side.

"Cem get back to the village," I said. "Find Tommy's people and tell them where we are. If you betray us, I'll find you and make you wish you hadn't."

Farkas darted forward, swiping the daggers at Tommy, who was the closer of the two of us. I blasted Farkas in the chest with a torrent of air, but he wrapped himself in a shield of air himself, and the two cancelled each other out.

Farkas flipped away from Tommy and I, putting distance between us again.

"He doesn't use his magic offensively," I whispered to Tommy as, out of the corner of my eye, Cem bolted into the forest. "He's all about speed and agility, about being defensive."

Tommy gave me a subtle nod.

"Why'd you kill Mona?" I asked him.

"Viktor told us that he wanted Varol to watch his loved one die," Farkas said. "Apparently, Viktor didn't like other people playing with his toys."

"Oh, I do not like you," I told him. "Tommy, go make sure Cem gets back in one piece."

"You sure?" Tommy asked.

"Yep, Farkas and I are going to have a chat." I hadn't taken my eyes off the assassin from the moment he'd arrived. "Get everyone into the castle, make sure no one leaves. Do you know about the werelions attacking?"

Farkas smiled. "You figured that out too? That was all Viktor, nothing to do with us. We kill the four, we get paid and go. With Viktor's passing, there was no one to pay us. I relayed that information to the lions by the way. They should be dealing with their hatred shortly."

Tommy clapped me on the shoulder. "Kill him quick."

"You seem very sure of yourself," Farkas said. "Am I meant to know who you are?"

I shrugged and ignited a whip of fire in one hand, and

a sword of flame in the other. "You'll find out," I told him, and dashed forward, bringing the whip around to flick toward his face, trying to close the gap between us as quickly as possible.

The assassin moved back at speed, and pushed his hand forward, catching me in a telekinetic blast that was strong enough to push me back several feet.

"You're the one who scrubbed the clone guys mind of you," I said, rolling my shoulders.

"I did," he admitted. "He was the newest, the most unknown. No way I would have done it to the others, kind of wish I had though, if one of them betrayed me."

"Ah, if it helps, they didn't do it voluntary," I told him. "They died pretty easily though."

Farkas' eyes narrowed in anger.

"You're going to have to find new people," I said. "Well, you won't, you're going to be dead in a few seconds."

Making Farkas angry did the trick and he ran toward me, his dual basilisk-tooth blades flashing through the air, trying to find my flesh as I deflected attack after attack, using air and fire magic to push his arms and the blades aside as we danced around the clearing.

One of the blades nicked the back of my hand, and I blasted Farkas in the chest with a palm of air magic, throwing him back across the clearing.

"You are not fighting," Farkas said, getting back to his feet.

"I'm trying to figure out a way to not have to kill you," I said. "I'm guessing that you're responsible for a lot of murders over the years, and frankly, I'd like to have the names." I didn't say anything about how taking the spirit of someone who can use mind magic is neither pleasant, nor advisable. Their minds are a mess, and I'd done it a few times and resolved never to do so again.

"You're not going to be able to take me alive," Farkas said with a laugh. "You're going to die out here for your friends to find, and then, once the werelions have murdered everyone in that castle, I'll be going home a rich man."

"You sure about that?"

He threw one of the basilisk-tooth blades at me, and I moved to dodge, but it followed me, Farkas' telekinesis making the blade track me like a homing missile. Tendrils of shadow leapt out of the ground, taking hold of the blade's hilt and tossing it aside.

"You can't do that," Farkas raged. He swiped his blade at me, and I moved to his side, driving my elbow into his ribs, before turning and following up with a knee to the exact same place.

Farkas' breath left his body in a grunt, and I drove a blade of lightning into his stomach, twisting it as I plucked the basilisk-tooth blade from his hand. I removed the blade of lightning and kicked Farkas in the chest, sending him sprawling to the ground.

"I helped kill a dragon not that long ago," I told Farkas. "I killed Kay, I beat Gilgamesh, I beat Apollo within an inch of his life. What do you think you can do to me, Farkas? You hunt from the shadows; you kill from the shadows." I crouched beside him. "I am the shadows."

Shadows poured over Farkas like a tsunami, and he bucked and screamed. I couldn't drag Farkas down into my shadow realm, he was a sorcerer, and that wouldn't work, but that didn't mean they were useless as a weapon. I turned dozens into razor-sharp spikes, which rammed into Farkas like he was a pin cushion, his scream of pain muffled by the shadows swarming his face.

With a wave of my hands, the shadows vanished.

Farkas was on all fours, blood pouring from a dozen

places as he tried to crawl away. I walked after him, a blade of fire in one hand.

"Please," he said. "I'll tell you everything. I have a notebook, I have details of every killing, all of them. I'll give it to you. I promise, just let me go."

"Where is it?" I asked him softly.

"My house in Budapest," he said. "Please."

I kicked him in the face hard enough to break his jaw and knock him out. I used my air magic to hogtie him, and dragged him over to Sorcery, who had remained just outside of the clearing, watching, and as calm as the day is long.

"We're going to take this sack of crap back," I said, replacing my air magic with actual rope that hung from Sorcery's saddle.

Sorcery looked at me, and then immediately froze, her gaze on the other side of the clearing. The darkness of the dense woodland hid whatever was there.

I reached out with my air magic, picking up heartbeats from the trees. Not just a dozen, but dozens and dozens of heartbeats. The werelions. The heartbeats were fast, they were ready for a fight. I climbed onto Sorcery just as the werelions burst from their hiding place, war cries upon their lips.

"Go," I said to Sorcery and she sprinted back through the forest, the sounds and smells of the horde behind us, driving her forward.

Sorcery knew this track and she raced, sure-footed, the sound of her hoofbeat and snorts of breath soon drowning out the sounds of our pursuers. I didn't dare look behind me. We reached the village, and I risked a look behind me, but there was nothing there. None of the werelions had followed us out of the forest. I looked up at the dusk colored skies.

"Nate," Remy said running over. "Tommy came back,

said we're about to be under attack."

"This is the arsehole who lead the assassins," I told Remy as Sorcery trotted through the village. I saw the stable-hand and climbed down from the tusked-horse. "Werelions are coming," I told him. "Get the tusked-horses to safety."

"Where?" The stable-hand asked, clearly scared as I spotted dozens of people being shepherded into the castle.

"In the castle," I said. "I don't care who complains, I'm not leaving them for werelion fodder. How long will you need?"

"Ten minutes," he said, flustered.

"You've got five," I said and knocked out Farkas again as he began to come around. I dragged him from the back of Sorcery and dumped him unceremoniously on the ground at Remy's feet.

"So, you've been productive," Remy said, poking Farkas with his foot.

"More is yet to come, we need to get everyone into that castle," I told him. "There are at least fifty werelions coming this way."

"Fifty?" Remy asked. "Great, just what the day needed."

Remy ran off and I left Farkas in the hands of several of Tommy's people as I spotted Tommy himself running toward me, Victoria being helped along by Lex.

"The poison still in her system?" I asked when Tommy arrived.

"No idea," he said.

I told him how many werelions there were.

"That's not good," Tommy said. "But there are a lot more of us than them, so I'm not sure just how much damage they think they can do. Waiting for nightfall isn't going to do them any good either."

"I guess we'll find out soon," I said as Lex and Victoria arrived.

"Do you know who killed Viktor?" Lex asked me.

"Yes," I told her. I was pretty sure I did, although now was hardly the time for that conversation. "Get in the castle, get Victoria somewhere safe. Somewhere guarded. Heavily."

Victoria looked over at me. "Is there a problem, Mister Garrett?"

"We're about to be attacked by several dozen were-lions," I said. "I doubt very much that they all belonged to Viktor's pride."

"He was joining prides with another from Hungary," she said.

"So I heard," I told her. "I think they want to expand outside of their own borders. Kill all of the competition, and you get free run of eastern Europe, and the Nordic countries."

There was a roar somewhere in the distance that made everyone stop and pay attention.

"My people are preparing for war," Lex said. "They will come in armor, and with weapons. This pride does not fight just in their werebeast forms. They will use silver. They have little honor."

"Well, they were going to murder you all during lunch, so honor is probably not something they worry about too much," I told her, and Lex and Victoria were hurried into the castle.

I looked over and saw several of the stable-hands leading in tusked-horses. Good.

"We going inside?" Tommy asked. There were still a lot of people heading into the castle, and I wasn't sure how long they had.

Remy, Diana, and Sky came and stood with Tommy and me. "We do this together," Diana said as more roars broke out in the darkness of the forest, and the last embers of light died.

CHAPTER TEN

The first werelions to attack ran over the drawbridge directly in front of where Remy, Diana, Tommy, Sky, and I stood. They were a snarling mass of werebeast. All claws and teeth in a din of noise. They wore leather armor, the runes bright in the darkness, and as the moonlight glinted off the weapons they held, it was obvious they hadn't just come to fight, but to butcher and kill.

I put up a barrier of air, and the moment the first wave hit it, I dumped lightning into it, throwing at least a few of the werelions back, but no one else stopped, even those who had caught fire from the lightning. They ignored the flames as Tommy and Diana took the fight to them.

Sky and Remy stood to one side of me, Remy with his swords drawn, and Sky holding her soul weapons—physical manifestations of her necromancy—a long dagger and a tomahawk axe, both shimmering blue. Soul weapons don't physically hurt people, they cause damage to the soul, killing without leaving a mark.

A large werelion, covered in armor, and with a battle-axe that was probably half my height, charged toward me. He swung down at my head, and I darted forward, stabbing him in the stomach with a blade of fire, the runes on his armor flashing as they stopped working. He kicked me in the chest, sending me flying back, but I anchored myself with air magic, and landed on my feet only a dozen feet away. The expression on the werelion's face suggested he'd expected something different to happen.

More werelions managed to dart around the five of us, and run into Tommy's people who were holding the line in the courtyard behind us. Tommy didn't employ idiots, so I knew they'd be able to take care of themselves.

The werelion in front of me started a slow, methodical walk, swinging the silver bladed axe from side to side as if it was meant to terrify me, or something. I created a blade of lightning in one hand and held it down to the ground, the tip crackling as it touched the snow.

The werelion went from walking to sprinting in the space of a step, and shadows leapt out of the ground, wrapping around his feet, tripping him. He roared as he fell forward, and tried to swipe at the shadows with one massive claw, but the second his attention was turned, I slammed the blade of lightning into the top of his skull and detonated the magic inside him.

If the blade itself hadn't killed him, the magic tearing him in half from the waist down, probably did. But just to be sure, I picked up the axe and buried it in what remained of his head.

"There are a lot more of them than fifty," Remy shouted as I walked past him, while he removed one of his swords from the skull of an enemy.

"I was on horseback riding away from them," I said. "Next time I'll stop and make them take a census."

"That's all I ask," Remy said as even more werelions ran toward us.

"I had no idea any pride was this bloody big," Tommy shouted, avoiding the swipe of a sword, before plunging his own up into the werelion's throat.

I threw balls of flame and lightning at anything that moved, but Tommy was right, this was a pride bigger than I'd anticipated. They must have been a hundred strong. There were wolfpacks with less numbers.

Tommy took off toward the fighting in the courtyard, with Remy and Sky behind him as the numbers rushing toward us thinned, mostly avoiding me to try and climb the walls of the castle. I dragged a few down with air magic, but as I couldn't find Diana, I didn't want to rush off and leave her to whatever she was facing. I raised a shield of air and scanned the area for her.

As I should have known, I needn't have worried. A hut wall exploded as a werelion crashed through it at high speed, an exceptionally pissed off Diana in full werebear form storming after it as she tossed aside the head of a second werelion.

The werelion got to his feet and looked at me, as if asking for help.

I shrugged.

It turned back to Diana, just as she punched it in the face hard enough that I heard the bones shatter even from twenty feet away. Werelions were stronger than werewolves, but werebears were in an entirely different league of strength. I'd have felt sorry for the werelion, had it not been trying to murder innocent people.

I turned back to the mass inside the courtyard, the sounds of fighting, the screams of pain mixed in with roars and howls from those there.

"Are you leaving?" A voice behind me asked.

I turned to see a man of about forty, walk toward me across the bridge. He wore a large fur coat that, considering it still had the animal's head attached, had once belonged to a grey wolf. He was white, over six feet tall, with broad shoulders, along which sat the aforementioned grey wolf hide.

"And you would be?" I asked.

"I am the leader of this pride," he told me. "My name is Demetri."

"Well, Demetri, your people are going to lose," I told him. "You have no element of surprise, you have no financial gain to still be here, either. Viktor is dead."

"I know," Demetri said. "This is about more than being paid, it's about making my pride the biggest in Eastern Europe. It's about making my pride a world power."

"It's about killing people who disagree with you," I said.

"That too," Demetri admitted as I spotted Diana slowly move toward him.

"Viktor told you about Kozma and Varol, and you figured you could use his hatred of the people here to clear out a whole lot of competition."

"I've been absorbing prides into my own," Demetri said. "Lex was offered the chance to join, and she turned me down. This is what happens to people who turn me down. Who turns down progress?"

"You're going to lose," I told him. "There are too many defenders."

"I don't need you all dead," Demetri said. "But enough of Lex's family will be dead, and that will satisfy me. It will cripple her pride; it will give us the edge."

Diana rushed Demetri, who ducked underneath her jab, and drove his elbow into her stomach, following up with a punch to her jaw that cracked her head to one side with vicious speed. Before I could move, he drove his knee into Diana's head, and I blasted him with air, sending him back into the hut that Diana had almost destroyed only moments ago.

Diana got back to her feet, shaking her head. "He's fast. He's not a werelion."

"What is he?" I asked her.

"I think we're about to find out," she told me as Demetri walked out of the hut. The fur was gone now, and he wore only leather trousers. He rubbed a hand over his muscular stomach, and then ran it through his long black hair.

There were shouts and screaming coming from the castle.

"Nate you got this?" Diana asked me.

I nodded without taking my eyes off the pride leader. "Go help," I told her.

"You shouldn't have sent her away," Demetri said.

"You shouldn't have gotten up this morning," I told him. "I guess we've both made mistakes."

"I don't know who you think you are, but you're going to die here," he said.

"My name is Nathan Garrett," I told him.

He shrugged. "I guess you're not as famous as you think."

"Farkas said the same thing," I told him as we began to circle each other at a distance. "It didn't work out so well for him."

"I'm not Farkas," the man said, and changed into a his weretiger beast form.

Weretigers were rare and dangerous, almost as strong as werebears, and almost as fast as werewolves.

"A weretiger leading werelions," I said. "Never heard of that."

"I don't care what I lead," Demetri said. "I care how

much power I can amass."

Demetri was nearly two feet taller than me and out-weighed me by several hundred kilograms. Weretigers were dense, heavy creatures, with a thick hide, and claws that I'd seen personally tear through metal. I rolled my shoulders and sighed. Today sucked.

I threw a ball of fire at Demetri, and clicked my fingers, causing it to explode as he darted aside, showering him in the remains of flame. Demetri ignored the flames, changed direction, and closed the gap between us in a second. He barreled into me, his claws raking along my chest as I kicked out and leapt back.

The thick jacket I'd been wearing was shredded, and I'd managed to get a shield of air up in time to stop Demetri from dis-emboweling me, but there were still three red welts on my chest where his claws had raked.

I removed the tattered jacket and tossed it aside, doing the same to the t-shirt beneath.

"You're no one impressive," Demetri said. "I've killed sorcerers before. You will be no different."

I said nothing as I created a blade of lighting. Shadows leapt from the ground, but Demetri was already moving faster than they could track him, and I was forced to duck one of his punches, and block another, which made my arm sting and lifted me off my feet.

"Stronger than you," he said, kicking out at me.

I dodged aside and drove the blade of fire down toward his leg, but he'd already moved out of the way.

"Faster than you," he said, his attitude superior and cocky.

He moved toward me again, and I blocked a punch, pushed aside a jab that was only there to think he was leaving himself open for a counterattack, and kicked him in the knee before he could kick out at me. I stepped toward him, intent on keeping up the attack, but he spun back and caught me in the chest with his boot, sending me up against the wall of a hut.

"Better than you," Demetri said with a smile.

I shrugged, cracked my knuckles, and readied myself into a fighting stance.

Demetri covered the distance between us in a moment, throwing a jab-cross combination, which I easily blocked and avoided, before he followed up with a knee, that I simply side-stepped. With my air magic activated, I was much faster, probably not weretiger fast, but it would hopefully keep me from getting kicked in the face.

I stepped around Demetri and punched him in the side of the head. He tried to backhand me, but I put some distance between us, and winked.

"Nice trick," Demetri said. "That's going to cost you."

"You talk a lot."

Demetri rushed me, moving much faster than he had before, and it took everything I had to keep him from catching me with his claws. I kept tracking back toward the courtyard where the fighting was still intense. I threw fire and air magic at Demetri as I moved and blocked, but he just ignored it and continued the assault, until he finally caught me with a punch to the side of the head that knocked me silly for just the right amount of time for him to drive his knee into my ribs and bring an elbow down into my temple, sending me sprawling to the snowy ground.

Demetri placed a foot on my chest and pushed down, and I gasped as the air was driven from my lungs.

"Is this the best you've got?" Demetri shouted to the heavens, and I saw that the wooden door to the castle had been broken open, the fighting having spilled into the castle, while only a half dozen werelions stood in the courtyard, cheering

Demetri's victory.

Demetri reached down and pulled me to my feet, lifting me off the ground by my throat, my feet dangling in the air.

"Do you have anything to say?" he asked, his breath warm on my face.

"I was hoping for a bigger crowd of your arsehole friends," I said.

"Why?" Demetri asked. "Do you need an audience to die?"

"Because people tend to stop fighting when they realize they can't win," I said, my voice hoarse as Demetri's one-handed grip on my neck tightened.

"This was fun," Demetri said. "I wish I could keep you as a pet."

I drove a dagger of lighting into Demetri's armpit, twisted it as he released his grip, and then extended it into a long blade, that almost removed his arm from the shoulder.

Demetri screamed as he moved back, blood pouring from the wound.

I used one of my own spirit weapons—a battle axe— and drove it into his stomach, which caused him to cry out as he threw himself back to put some distance between us.

"This isn't a fight you can win," I told him as I created a sphere of air in one palm, spinning it faster and faster as I added my lightning and fire magic to it, until it was the side of my hand.

"I had you beat," Demetri said, jumping toward me, the claws on the end of his one good arm, out to catch me. I snapped forward, and drove the sphere up into his exposed chest, releasing the magic that threw him fifty feet up into the air. He hit the ground with an unpleasant splat.

He got back to his feet as I drove a blade of fire into his

ribs, twisted the blade when he took a half-hearted swipe at me, and detonated the magic.

Demetri was engulfed in flames, and the smell of burning flesh and fur filled the air around me. He dropped to his knees and screamed, so I extinguished the flames and turned back to the half dozen werelions who were watching the fight with wide eyes and open mouths.

"Surrender or you're all next," I told them.

"You're not a normal sorcerer," Demetri said. "That power."

"My name is Nathan Garrett," I whispered. "You might know me as Hellequin."

The name clearly meant something to him, as Demetri looked up at me with genuine fear in his eyes. "I'm so sorry," Demetri said.

"Fuck your sorry," I told him and drove a blade of lighting into his ear, detonating the magic inside his skull.

I turned to the werelions who were still watching. "Who's next?" I shouted.

They all dropped to their knees, hands on their heads, and changed back into their human forms.

"Good fucking choice," I said, as I walked past them into the castle.

CHAPTER ELEVEN

Any werelions who were directly inside the castle foyer and had seen me kill Demetri had surrendered immediately. I found twenty werelions on their knees, just like their friends in the courtyard.

The fighting was over pretty quickly after that. The werelions who had been inside the castle hadn't seen his death, but Tommy, Diana, Remy, Sky, and everyone else who was there were more than a match for the werelions once the wedding guests had joined in.

There were close to forty werelion prisoners by the time we finished, and they were all marched outside of the castle, forced to wear a sorcerer's band to stop them accessing their powers. They would wait for Avalon to arrive and take them for whatever punishment was deemed appropriate.

The prisoners were marched past Demetri's corpse, who had been decapitated by Remy when he'd gone outside and sworn he'd seen the weretiger move. Personally, I just thought he wanted to make sure, which wasn't something I was against.

Tommy's contacts in Avalon arrived and arrested everyone involved, promising that the werelions and Farkas would be dealt with accordingly. I hoped that would be the case, but it's hard to think the worst in people, so I made a mental note to check up on what happened to everyone.

When it was over, I found the stable-hand who'd been leading Sorcery and checked that she was okay, along with everyone else.

"She kicked a werelion in the face so hard that I have to clean brain matter off her hooves," the stable-hand told me.

"Good girl," I said, picking an apple from the bushel and giving it to her as I scratched her behind the ear.

"They're easy to grow affection toward, aren't they?" The stable-hand said. "It's why I like working with them so much."

"Take care," I paused. "I'm sorry, I never got your name."

"Arthur," he told me.

"Like the king," I said.

He nodded. "He's returned now, hasn't he? You think he can bring order to everything?"

"I really hope so," I said. "Take care of yourself."

I rejoined everyone in the castle and told Tommy's people to get Melody, Sven, Beth, Logan, Lex, and Victoria to the dining hall, but to let them all shower and change first. There was blood all over the floor and walls of the castle, so I doubted anyone was in their best dress, and didn't want them to have to sit around with their own, or someone else's blood on them.

"You think the wedding is going ahead?" Sky asked me.

"I hope so, we'll see after I tell the main players who killed Viktor."

"One of them did it, didn't they?" Sky said. "I knew they were a bunch of double-crossing assholes."

I smiled. "You're more than welcome to watch. In fact,

depending on what happens, I might actually need some help."

Gordon and Matthew walked around the corner at that moment. Both were covered in blood, and both looked like they'd had a long night.

I told them about the dining hall.

"An hour," Matthew said.

"You planning on washing up yourself?" Gordon asked.

I looked down at my own bloody hands. "Probably a good idea. How many did we lose tonight?"

"Twenty-seven," Matthew said sadly. "Ten guests, seventeen villagers. None of Tommy's people, thankfully, but some of the werelions managed to climb the castle to the rooms above and started going to town up there. It's not pretty, Nate. I'm glad Demetri is dead, or we'd have to execute him anyway."

"I can see if I can bring back his spirit for you to destroy," Sky said absentmindedly.

"You can do that?" Gordon asked.

Sky shrugged nonchalantly. "Sure."

"Remind me to never piss you off," Gordon said with a slight bow of his head.

Sky smiled and winked at him.

Diana and Tommy were directing traffic just beyond the foyer of the castle. His people had pretty much saved this realm from a massacre, and no one was stupid enough to argue with him about it.

"Heard you're having your Poirot moment," Diana said to me.

"I was thinking more Colombo," I said.

"You do annoy people," Tommy pointed out. "It's like your superpower."

117

"Both of you are terrible people," I said. "I could have been anywhere right now, but instead, I decided to come help you, Tommy. And I'll remind you of that fact for a long time."

Tommy dropped to his knees. "Is this better?"

"You mock me," I said in mock indignation. "Good day to you, sir."

Tommy got back to his feet as Diana slapped me on the back. "Glad to have you here."

"I said, good day," I shouted, turning as if to storm away, before looking back at them both. "I'm glad I was here. I'm glad you're all safe."

Tommy removed a piece of paper from his pocket and passed it to me. "I think you might find this interesting."

I unfolded the paper and smiled. "Where'd you get it?"

"Viktor's room," Tommy said.

"Thanks very much for that."

I went to shower, watching the hot water go from red to pink, and finally translucent took any built-up adrenaline with it. I dressed in a dark suit and a white shirt, because they were literally the only items of clothing I still owned that didn't need a wash. I'd expected to be in the realm for a few days, I hadn't expected to be fighting a pride of werelions, a weretiger, and assassins. People often suggested that trouble followed me wherever I went, and honestly, it was looking more and more like they had a valid point.

An hour later, I made my way to the dining hall. Everyone I'd asked to be there was sat on chairs facing the windows. Several of Tommy's guards stood at the doors, and Matthew, Gordon, Sky, Remy, Diana, and Tommy were all among the guests. I was pretty sure should trouble break out, it was going to be the shortest in history.

"Ladies and gentlemen," I said as I walked across the hardwood floor. "Thank you all for coming."

"Can the wedding continue?" Sven asked.

"Probably," I said.

"We were told to come here, but no one told us why," Melody said. Of all of them, she was the one who'd taken the opportunity to shower and change as an invitation to dress up. She looked like she was going out for a party in 1920s America, in her long green dress and black heels. Everyone else wore normal street clothes, apart from Sven who had donned another suit.

"This won't take long," I assured them when I got to the front of the group. "I wanted to let you all know that Viktor was behind the murders in the forest. It appears that Victoria was meant to be unhurt, allowed to flee and take word of what had happened. Viktor had a list of people he wanted dead." I removed the paper Tommy had found and unfolded it. "He kept a list of orders in his room, I assume because he was concerned of being screwed over by Farkas or Demetri and his werelions. The orders were signed by all three men, agreeing to the terms set out."

"What were the terms?" Beth asked.

"Victoria was to be allowed to flee back to the village," I said. "It was to stoke fear. Melody and Sven were to be butchered in their rooms, again to stoke fear, and then tonight, Demetri and his lions were going to kill the rest of you. Demetri and Viktor would rule the pride together, with Viktor being paid handsomely for setting this up."

I put the paper back in my pocket. "A young man found a possibility to get vengeance for his family, and he told Viktor, who used the opportunity to settle scores."

"The world is better off without him in it," Melody shouted.

"True, but that leads me to his murder," I said.

119

"I assume Demetri did it," Sven said.

"Maybe Viktor wanted more money," Lex called out.

"Victoria was hit by an arrow and infected with a paralyzing agent," I said. "The same agent used to silence Viktor. The same one that let him be carried to the stables and nailed to them. They cut off his feet because there are few things worse for a were than the loss of the ability to run. He felt all of it, he just couldn't vocalize the agony that was caused."

"And you killed Demetri," Lex said.

"Demetri didn't kill Viktor," I said. "Farkas didn't either. The problem is that none of the other victims in the woods had manticore venom in them. So, if you'll indulge me, I'll tell you what I think happened."

No one said anything, nor did they move.

"The plan to kill Viktor was concocted before the invitations were sent," I began. "This was the perfect time. This was how everyone's lives could be made better. Sven, you two hated either other and he wanted you dead. Melody, you cheated on him, he was a thug, a bully, abusive, and generally just a shitty person. Lex, you just couldn't stand what he was doing to Melody. Victoria, you always hated his guts. Beth and Logan, neither of you liked him, and both of you would have been happy to see him gone. You didn't want him at the wedding, but Sven convinced you both to invite him anyway. But not his pack.

"I think when Victoria got attacked, she used the opportunity to apply the paralyzing agent to her body before reaching us. She either left it in the woods to be found by whoever was meant to give it to Viktor, or you got into the medical hut first and used the time to dab a bit on the wound, but you used too much and it almost knocked you out for the day.

"I think Sven applied the paralyzing agent, probably in a drink you gave to Viktor. He trusted that you would be the good guy, he was going to have you murdered, and there's no way he thought you were doing the same to him. Once he was out, several of you murdered him. I don't know exactly who did what, but you all took part. You were removing a murderous arsehole, so you had your turn, Orient Express style."

"Interesting hypothesis," Victoria said.

"But you can't prove anything," Beth said, getting to her feet.

"Nor do I plan to," I told them. "I said I wanted the truth, and I did, and I have it. You all helped murder Viktor because he was an evil little shit. This isn't human law, this isn't even Avalon law, and I've certainly killed people for being less of an asshole than Viktor was. Besides, he was going to have you all murdered at your wedding, so fuck him."

"So, we're good here?" Melody said, getting to her feet.

"Not quite," I said. "Victoria how'd you get the paralyzing agent?"

"Kozma had it on him," Victoria said, looking up at me and holding my gaze. "I grabbed his trousers when I ran. I didn't want it to be found if we all died. It would have put the plan in jeopardy."

Lex held Victoria's hand and squeezed.

"You all conspired to murder, and in some cases, took part in the murder, of a monstrous man during a wedding celebration," I said. "Why'd you ask specifically for Tommy?"

"Because he's good at his job," Logan said.

"You knew he'd want to figure out what happened," I said.

"We'd have told him," Sven said, looking over at Tommy. "But when the murders happened, we couldn't risk anyone trying to stop us. Viktor had to die."

"And with Demetri and Viktor gone, you now have access to a large part of Eastern Europe," Tommy said.

"That was never the plan," Lex told him.

"But a happy coincidence anyway," Sky said.

"If that's how you want to look at it," Lex told her.

"This is the most fucked-up wedding I've ever been to," Remy said. "Honestly, you can't make this shit up."

"You can all go," I said. "I suggest you have your wedding and leave a gigantic tip for everyone who works here. And I'm talking six figures. I don't have a problem with you killing Viktor, but you brought a murderer to these people's lives, and they didn't deserve that. Make it right."

"We will," Logan said, offering me his hand, which I shook.

"Don't make me ever regret letting you all go," I told them as they all walked away.

When the room emptied except for me and my friends, I sat on one of the chairs and sighed.

"So, this was fun," Remy said. "Remind me how much I'm getting paid for this?"

"I thought you were doing it as a favor," Tommy said.

"Yes, until we almost got murdered," Remy said. "Being eaten automatically kicks in the Remy doesn't want to be fucking murdered fund."

"I have a similar fund," Diana said.

"See, standard operating procedure," Remy said with a smile.

"At least it wasn't boring," I said.

"That is true," Sky said from behind me. "Hopefully

nothing this exciting will happen for a while. I could do with a holiday. Somewhere warm. Without weddings."

"Thanks for coming," Tommy said, seriously. "All of you. It meant a lot. And my people are alive partly because of you guys."

"Tommy," Gordon said. "If you hadn't been here, a lot of people would be dead."

"Possibly us among them," Matthew said.

"It was good to see you both," I said. "Even with the death, mayhem, and general…" I waved my hands around. "Everything."

We sat and talked for a while, before heading to bed. The next morning, the wedding took place quickly and most of the guests elected to return home rather than stay in a castle where some of their number had been murdered.

I congratulated the married couple but said nothing else to anyone who had been involved in what had happened. I knew they weren't responsible for what Viktor and Demetri had done, but I was still ticked off that I'd gone to a wedding and ended up having to kill a bunch of people.

As I left the castle, Tommy was waiting for me. "Hey," I said.

"Cem died last night," Tommy told me. "He threw himself at a werelion to keep him from killing a young family who were here for the wedding. He saved their lives. I thought you'd like to know."

I sighed; I was conflicted about how I felt. On the one hand Cem had helped cause what had happened, but on the other he'd done it because all he'd wanted was justice for his family, and I could understand that.

"I'm glad I came," I said as we walked through the courtyard.

"Seriously?" Tommy said.

"We helped save lives, that's more important than me being irritated that I didn't have a quiet weekend."

Tommy laughed. "I'll make sure the next one is much quieter."

"You got plans?"

"I'm going to go home and give my wife and daughter a hug," Tommy said. "I hope we get a few years of quiet now."

"Me too," I said. "You know if you ever need me, I'll be there. No matter what."

Tommy hugged me. "I know."

"But if you ever invite me to a wedding where you're doing security, you need to bring a lot more security. Like, all of the security."

Tommy nodded. "I will."

"Say hi to Olivia and Kase for me," I told him. "I'm going to go sleep."

Tommy headed back toward the castle. I'd had worse weekends, but I hoped the battle in The Realm of Dreich would be the last one I'd need to take part in for the foreseeable future. But knowing my luck, something much bigger was on the horizon, waiting for me to be content, to find that little bit of peace, before it jumped out to surprise me.